BETS AND SCAMS

FOR L

About the Author

Gary Schwartz is a leading authority on Dutch painting of the seventeenth century and publishes and lectures on the subject in the United States, Holland and Israel. His books on Rembrandt (Penguin, 1985) and Pieter Saenredam (Thames and Hudson, 1990) are standard texts on these two very different masters. Schwartz has pioneered a new approach to artistic biography and is an outspoken critic of connoisseurs who attempt to establish the corpus of an artist without taking account of historical circumstances.

Schwartz was born in Brooklyn, NY, in 1940 and is a graduate of Johns Hopkins University and the Hebrew University of Jerusalem. He has lived in the Netherlands since 1965. *Bets and Scams* is his first novel.

GARY SCHWARTZ

BETS AND SCAMS

A Novel of the Art World

Marion Boyars
New York ▪ London

First published in the United States and Great Britain in 1996
by Marion Boyars Publishers
237 East 39th Street, New York, N.Y. 10016
24 Lacy Road, London, SW15 1NL

Distributed in Australia and New Zealand by
Peribo Pty Ltd, 58 Beaumont Road, Mount Kuring-gai, NSW 2080

First published in Dutch translation in 1994
under the title *Dutch Kills*

Library of Congress Cataloging-in-Publication Data
Schwartz, Gary, 1940–
  [Dutch kills. English]
  Bets and Scams : a novel of the art world /Gary
Schwartz.
  I. Title.
PT5881.29.C594D8813   1995
813'.54--dc20   95-19678

British Library Cataloguing in Publication Data
Schwartz, Gary
  Bets and Scams : Novel of the Art World
  I. Title
  839.31364 [F]

ISBN 0–7145–3008–5

Typeset in 12½/13½pt Garamond Condensed and Erie by
Ann Buchan (Typesetters), Shepperton
Printed on acid-free paper by
Redwood Books, Trowbridge, Wiltshire

'Is this Mitchell Fleishig?'

'Yes, who are you?'

'You don't need to know who I am. All you need to know is that I am calling on behalf of the Angelo Credit Corporation. Mr. Fleishig, you have run out of time.'

'Hey, come on! What is this? I spoke to Benny before the weekend, and he said I should take a month to get the best quote I could. Do some comparison selling, he said. He's going to do the same. The story line is, at the end of the month, we're going to compare notes and either go for the best deal or he'll take title.'

'That was the story line before the weekend. In the meanwhile, Mr. Santangelo has made some calls, and now he has decided not to wait until the end of the month. He wants the full amount of your loan now.'

'I think I better talk to him again.'

'He doesn't want to talk to you, Mr. Fleishig. If I were you, I wouldn't try to get him on the phone. He is very angry at you. He found out that you were trying to fuck him over.'

'What? What? What are you talking about? Mr. Santangelo and I went over the collection together, and the prices, and the situation. Everybody holding art has gotten burned. He knows that. We're going to cut our losses, and I will make good on the difference. Down to the last penny, with every cent of interest. We talk timetable at the end of the month. That's an agreement.'

'That is no longer an agreement. That was an agreement as long as Mr. Santangelo thought that you were the innocent victim of the collapse of the art market. He is full of understanding for innocent victims. But now he has found out that *he* is the innocent victim of a scam. He found out that you borrowed a million and a half dollars from him on goods that aren't worth shit. They weren't worth shit before the market fell, and they won't be worth shit after it recovers.'

'What are you saying? That's a load of crap. Those are signed original old master paintings in good condition. Mr. Santangelo knows that.'

'What Mr. Santangelo knows is that the artists who made those paintings are not bankable. And you told him they *were* bankable. He spoke to some mavens who never heard of them. One of the biggest art sellers in Los Angeles never even heard of the city they come from.'

'Who did he talk to? Who told him that? That's crazy. They're a little specialized, but the Utrecht school is top quality. You just have to know something about the history, about the market.'

'If you know so much about the market, you sell the paintings. You have one week. And let me tell you something. Mr. Santangelo did not want to give you one week. He is giving you a week not as a favor to you, but as a favor to me. I asked for it on the chance that it might save me an unpleasant job. So you get a banker's check for one million eight hundred and twenty thousand dollars onto Mr. Santangelo's desk by next Tuesday morning, and you and I will never meet. Goodbye, Mr. Fleishig.'

On the bedroom wall of Lodewijk Altstad's apartment on East 78th Street hung a painting of a girl by the seventeenth-century Utrecht artist Jan van Bronchorst. Altstad also owned a second version of the composition, which he kept in the bedroom of his place in Amsterdam. They were virtually indistinguishable. Seeing them together, one would notice that the blue-green background in the New York version was shallower, even a bit shrill, and that the contours did not have the same decisiveness. Altstad thought it was a repetition by the master himself, a replica. With three thousand miles between the two pictures, the differences existed only in the mind of the one man who knew them both. The art dealer's waking routine began with an attribution at fifteen feet.

'Replica. New York. Still got the eye.'

Owning both versions of the composition gave Altstad a glow of good fortune, as if he were about to remember that it was his tenth birthday, or that before he went to sleep the Nobel Prize Committee had called to congratulate him.

The girl was different than other Utrecht school models. Honthorst and Baburen painted party girls, as exciting as the girls from Homemaking who used to drive Altstad crazy when he was in high school in Amsterdam. Painted girls in bonbonnière bodices showing the tops of big, soft boobs, with a plume or red-tongued tulip quivering in their hairdo, they enticed you with a broad, dimpled smile, stroking a dove, cupping a peach, plucking a lute. They looked so easy, you could not tell where the sarcasm in the painting came from, the warning. Is it because they showed their teeth? Grab me if you dare, you'll like it better than you dream, but you will pay more than you can afford. Depending on what the girl was after, you would be left stripped and robbed or enslaved as the husband in a housewife's home.

The girl in Altstad's Bronchorst was different. She was not dolled up but draped in heavy, formless violet-brown velvet covering a white linen shift with a finicky hem you wanted to take between your fingers. The right breast, perhaps supported slightly by her wrist, was bare to halfway the nipple, framing with her broad soft shoulder a fold like the vulva of a little girl. Her raven hair was all ringlets, enclosing her brow and temple in a gently rippled arc and rolling freely down her back. She had a long, straight nose, full lips closed expressionlessly, and bright black eyes, wide open but looking away.

This girl was not out to prick your libido into thoughtless action like the Honthorsts. (She was painted better, too. Why did she fetch only a quarter of a Honthorst price?) It was more as if she had just made love to you for the first time, unwisely but unforgettably. The painting perpetuated the moment when fulfillment was giving way to fresh desire. But now the girl was undecided. You had moved her more deeply than she expected, and she felt she had to choose between leaving the man she was going to marry or renouncing you at once. Altstad liked to think that she was the daughter of a patrician family sent to Bronchorst for an engagement portrait. She and the painter had fallen in love. He had dutifully finished the engagement portrait (where was it?), but had also painted two versions of a love portrait, one for each of them. Altstad did not know how the story ended. It rushed him every morning.

Altstad's apartment was on the fifth floor of a converted brownstone. The grime on the windows colored all light sepia and no longer registered rainstreaks. He could only tell what the weather was like by circumstantial evidence. Spotting a woman holding a fur collar tightly to her neck, Altstad put on a parka sweatshirt and long jogging pants. He checked himself for singles and keys, unbarred the steel door of the apartment, set the alarm, bolted the locks, and hit the streets, feeling a little less like a birthday boy.

He walked west, dimly aware of the wet mist and the street scene while images of Dutch paintings began to crowd his mind. Before he reached Madison he passed in and out of the turbulence of a Franciscus Xavery storm at sea he had sold to a partner in a brokerage firm. Lightning lit a ship bearing down on a rocky coast. Good luck to all hands. Crossing Madison, his head crackled with static from paintings for sale up and down the street. Speelberg had a painting of *Vashti stripping* that he was selling as a Drost. If it was good, the Old Testament freak Aarons would pay one-and-a-half times what Speelberg was asking. But Altstad thought it was a copy. If he bought it from Speelberg and sold it to Aarons, and Aarons later came to the same conclusion, he would lose his only customer in the Midwest outside Chicago.

In the left corner of his gaze the gilded naked bodies of a man and woman appeared, hovering over the entrance to the old Parke-Bernet building. He tried not to think of the auction at Old York that evening. Lot 34. Flemish School. Please God, let no one find out what he knew about lot 34. Why was that one box of photographs on the return plank at the Dutch Center for Art History in The Hague yesterday? The guest book had been signed by Gordon Rich, who was gone before Altstad arrived. If Rich knew, he would peddle the information to Speelberg for a quarter of the increment and finally begin to live up to his name. But he didn't know, he couldn't. Unless he had been tipped from London. Where was the fax from London?

At the corner of Fifth, he passed beneath the guns of the Institute of Fine Arts, where he had been made useless for any life except that of the art professional. Rubachev had tapped him and bullied him through the long ordeal. What would Rubachev have said about the van Bronchorsts and the Xavery? Never heard of either of them, absolutely. No one at the Institute knew much about Dutch painting when he was there. But every art historian had heard of the artist who painted lot 34 in this evening's auction.

Altstad had a thirty-hour day behind him, including the six

hours he picked up on the plane between Holland and New York. Ahead was a ten o'clock appointment at the Met. As he waded through the fumes of Fifth Avenue, between creeping bumpers, the museum hulked uninvited in his peripheral gaze. The sight brought with it a vision not of Rembrandt or Vermeer, but of the Jacques de Gheyn horse Altstad was going to try to sell in two hours.

Across Fifth Avenue and into the park, Altstad started pacing himself to the stride of another brisk walker, a woman no younger than himself, in black leotards and a headset she kept adjusting. He praised himself for his wisdom in not exerting himself on the first morning after a flight. In less than a minute he realized that he *was* exerting himself and that the woman was pulling away from him anyway, looking as relaxed as if she were walking down a shopping street in pumps. He kept the desperation off his face as he watched her in grim amazement. After the Park Drive, she kept walking west, which Altstad had been planning to do. Instead, he turned south toward the boathouse, thankful that he would never have to admit his humiliation to anyone else. Pulling himself along through the cold and dirty drizzle, he remembered Willem Molenaar's advice: whenever you see a customer, the weather is glorious. Under his breath (was he starting to hyperventilate?) he began to sing 'Good Day Sunshine'.

With two large styrofoam cups of coffee, two buttered rolls with fried eggs over, *The Wall Street Journal* and *The New York Times*, Altstad opened his front door slowly and walked gently across the hall. Although the one-and-a-half passenger elevator took longer than the stairs, he used it now, to avoid running into his landlady. Actually, Mrs. Hinsythe was not his landlady. She was a member of the old New York family which had once occupied the entire townhouse, but since she sold the building in 1968, for less than a fifth of what it was worth today, she rented. The owner of the building was Zalman Properties, which Mrs. Hinsythe had told him earnestly was named for an eighteenth-century wonder rabbi. The firm consisted of one person, the wife of a Crown Heights chassid, Saryl Krieger. After the sale and the conversion of the building, Mrs. Hinsythe kept the apartment that had been made out of her old front parlor on the second floor. Of course it was the most expensive apartment in the building, but she had to have it, and could just about afford it. She worshipped Mrs. Krieger for her superhuman ability to earn money out of a building that her own family, in the course of a century, had paid for many times over, in interest and upkeep alone. Mrs. Hinsythe worked without pay as the absentee landlady's eyes and ears.

Not that Altstad had anything to fear. His rent for the month was paid. It always was. Once he had been late, and Mrs. Krieger had called him about it, in a voice she reserved for delinquent tenants. Immediately after hanging up the phone, he had decided that from then on his payments to Mrs. Krieger would have priority over all others. First to fall by the wayside would be the statements from the credit card companies, which were designed to ease you into debt to begin with. But Mrs. Krieger also came before the utilities, the telephone company, the mortgage on his apartment in Amsterdam, and the Dutch and American tax collectors. He would hold off business partners and auction houses, ignore court orders and even cancel the monthly payments that kept his mother out of the nursing home. If all his credit was exhausted and he had no money at all, that was no problem either. He would rob a grocery store, and if he got caught he would commit suicide. The greatest certainty in his life was that he would never again give Mrs. Krieger cause to put on that voice, a voice which cut through human dignity like a chainsaw through flesh. That March morning he wondered how far down the list of preventive measures he would have to go in order to meet the next rent date in two weeks. A minor concern.

Over breakfast, Altstad took a look at last week's trading. He did not play the market, but most of his customers were locked into it in one way or another. The Dow was up eleven points, which should keep them cheery, on the average, until

Monday drinks. But the averages were not what counted. He checked the bank of the one board member of the Metropolitan Museum who collected Dutch paintings; Aarons' toy company; the car and parts manufacturers who had recently started funding Detroit acquisitions again; the Chicago department store chain whose retired president was after museum-quality pieces; the conglomerate that owned the brokerage house behind one of the great New York collections; the Dallas oilfield outfitters with four art foundations; Old York. Today he went straight for United Grains, which funded a classy museum in Houston. Down one and three-eighths, but still close to the twelve-month high. May the Lord give them a good week. To get the most out of the deal he hoped to do with the museum, he should be in partnership with a broker who knew how to bump the price of Ugrain.

Skimming the *Journal*, he was stopped by an item on an insider trading charge connected with the Cybotics takeover. This probably accounted for the money that his newest client had been spending, but meant that he wouldn't be hearing from him for a while. He had finally found a buyer for Catholic allegories, and the man had to get himself caught with his hand in the till.

For news about Altstad's biggest customer, neither the *Times* nor the *Journal* was any help, and the *Hollywood Reporter* was not sold on Madison Avenue. Shares in Mitchell Fleishig's company, Rodeo Realty, may have been traded over lunch at the Polo Club, but there wasn't a stock exchange that would touch them. He was glad he didn't have an appointment with Fleishig on this trip.

Altstad showered, shaved and dressed. At 9:30 he called the *Kensington Journal* in London and asked for the editor-in-chief.

'Hello, Georgine, it's Lodewijk.'

'Lodewijk, how wonderful that you're calling. I have terrific news for you.'

That was really all that Altstad had to hear. The flush of victory began at his forehead and traveled down his frame during the rest of the conversation.

'Our reader could not have been more enthusiastic about your article. He said you had made a sensational find, and your arguments were absolutely incontrovertible. You know how impressed *I* was, but I'm no specialist, so I am smugly satisfied that my own judgment has been corroborated. Everyone here is delighted to have the article for the *Kensington*. We are going to put it up front in the May issue, so we're in a terrible rush. I sent it off for typesetting just before lunch. When can you fill in the information about the whereabouts of the painting?'

'That *is* wonderful news, Georgine. But please, please, keep it confidential for a while longer. If you fax me the galleys, I'll fill in the ownership on the proofs. I'm calling from New York.'

'I do not have to tell you, do I, that we never publish new attributions of paintings in the trade? This painting does not belong to you or another dealer by any chance?'

'Heaven forfend. The painting has been acquired by a well-known museum. They want things under wraps until the official announcement.'

'Right,' Georgine Eton said a bit doubtfully as she scribbled a note to her production man. 'I'll have the proofs faxed to you straight from the printers; they work a night shift, so the fax will go off tonight. When can I have your corrections?'

'How's the end of the week?'

'That's just perfect, Lodewijk. Thank you so awfully for your help.'

'The thanks are all mine, Georgine. But don't get angry if I tell you again how important it is that nothing of this gets out yet. Did you tell that to your reader and your editors and the printers?'

'Lodewijk, everything we publish is treated with the greatest confidentiality. But I'll repeat the instructions to all concerned.'

'Please pardon me for insisting. I know it must sound paranoid. But I need your absolute assurance. And I have a question. I know you can't tell me who your reader was, but can you tell me who it wasn't? It wasn't Gordon Rich, by any chance?'

'Oh no, what an idea! I wouldn't dream of trusting his opinion on an attribution. But it's good that you mention it. He has the habit of dropping in here from time to time and flirting with one of my editors. I will pass the word along that your article is to be kept strictly hidden from him.'

'Has he been around since my article was submitted?'

'You *are* a bit paranoid, aren't you? There really isn't anything to worry about. Your article will be in print in four weeks, and there is hardly any danger that anyone can get the attribution published anywhere else before then, is there?'

'I know, but still. *Has* he been around?'

'Let me think. You dropped off your manuscript and photos about three weeks ago. Gordon, Gordon, Gordon . . . . It could be. I recall him looking like something the cat dragged in, trying to smile at me with a cup of tea in his mouth. When was that rainstorm? What a question. It could have been any day in the past month. I think it was about two weeks ago. But you know, at that point I was the only one in the office who had read your article. I sent it to the reader myself. It came back the day before yesterday, and we discussed it at an editorial meeting this morning. Oh, by the way, the reader had some minor suggestions which we incorporated, along with a few small corrections of mine. Your English is so good. If we got anything wrong, just fix it up in the galleys.'

'You won't have gotten anything wrong, Georgine. You're the best. I've got to go. *Tot ziens*, love.'

At ten o'clock, Altstad checked his overcoat and strode in his double-breasted banker's stripe across the Great Hall of the Metropolitan Museum of Art to the information desk. The attendant dialed the extension of Frederick Auge and handed the receiver to Altstad. 'Are you in the hall, Mr. Altstad? I'll be right down.'

Altstad paced slowly, soaking up the atmosphere. No museum in Europe had an entrance hall to compete with this one. An outdoor staircase covering half the area of a city block led to a palatial *piano nobile* whose front room could house all of Gilded Age New York society at an opening. Visitors still felt transformed when they entered. Suburban matrons lived up effortlessly to the elevated setting, as if it were only their due. School classes would test the acoustics, but they were intimidated enough to behave the way humble visitors were intended to: impressed by the higher things in life, thankful that their betters were willing to share such beauty with them even if they were too ignorant to understand it. He thought of the corresponding space in the Rijksmuseum, which, although it could be reached only through cramped ground-floor entrances and less-than-grand staircases, had even loftier pretensions. The architect designed it as a portal to semi-divine revelation, a key to understanding how art mediates between man and God. He turned the view from the hall toward the *Night Watch* into the nave of a Gothic church. Later directors of the museum were so embarrassed or offended by this popery that they performed official acts of iconoclasm against it. They emasculated the program by removing or covering up murals and mosaics, painting the walls and ceiling white, neutralizing the space to the point that it no longer meant anything to anyone. The same directors, when unofficial acts of vandalism were performed against works of art in their care, invariably branded them acts of diseased minds. If you have to be deranged to damage a work of art, what about them? Altstad started when Auge touched his shoulder.

They climbed the broad central stairway and went straight into the European Paintings galleries. Although Auge was well past the official retirement age, he had no trouble with the stairs. Altstad remembered his seminars under Auge, marathon sessions that exhausted the students but which seemed to give the old man more energy as he went. Taking a detour, he led Altstad to the large companion portraits which had been early Rembrandt landmarks until the recent challenge to their authorship by the Netherlands Rembrandt Commission. Auge knew he did not have to introduce the subject to Altstad. He halted in front of the portraits and said, 'What do *you* think?' Altstad was relieved.

There were half a dozen other pictures in the same gallery whose Rembrandt labels he considered an insult to specialists and a shameless deception of the public. Had Auge asked him about one of those, their meeting would have gotten off to a bad start. The portraits were no problem.

'These paintings are dated 1632. That was Rembrandt's first year in Amsterdam. Even if he had a large studio from the start, he would still be training his assistants, in the middle of an incredibly busy schedule. Anyone who asks us to believe that Rembrandt would entrust a job as important and expensive as these portraits to untried helpers, and get work of this quality out of them, has to show more proof than the Commission has.'

'I'm glad you feel that way. But I don't think the historical argument is even necessary. Just look at those flesh tones and the modelling around the man's eyes. The modulation of the blacks in the costume is first class. You saw the autoradiographs. They did, too. I simply cannot understand it.'

With a snort, Auge moved on to the camouflaged doorway that let them into the Department of European Paintings and his office. They climbed over piles of books and papers to the curator's desk and the visitor's overstuffed wingchair. Altstad instinctively scanned the spines of the piled-up books. Most were museum and exhibition catalogues, with a bias towards Flemish art of the seventeenth century. This was no surprise; Auge's catalogue of Flemish paintings in the Met was long expected.

'I'm sorry I can't offer you coffee in my office, the way everyone does in Holland. Here you have to go down to the staff restaurant for a decent cup of coffee.'

'Going without ten o'clock coffee *is* one of the hardest adjustments a Dutchman has to make to the outside world, Dr. Auge. But I'll survive.'

'Before we go to Conservation, I wanted to ask you about ownership. Is there any problem with title, or with the export license?'

They want it, thought Altstad. He contained himself. 'The

seller is Willem Molenaar. Some other dealers may have part of the painting, but Molenaar is completely accountable. He bought it last year from Baron Achterhoofd in Den Bosch. An ancestor of his got it as a gift from King Willem I in 1827, when the ancestor opened an express coach service between The Hague and Brussels. Molenaar has a notarized statement from the Baron which comes with the painting. Export is no problem. There are less than two hundred paintings on the list of forbidden exports, and this is not one of them. It is not even likely to raise eyebrows, with the other version in the Rijksmuseum.'

'That sounds good. The simpler the better. I don't have to tell you what happened last year to my former colleague in French painting with his Poussin that was supposedly from Liechtenstein but actually came from a protected collection in Besançon. Half the French government did nothing for a week but insult us to the kind of newspapers and magazines they wouldn't deign to talk to about anything important. It's one of my strong points in proposing acquisitions that I have never gotten the museum involved in an affair of that kind. Any dealer who ever misrepresented the title or permissions situation to me would go on my well-publicized black list.'

Altstad let this speech — half declaration of piety and half threat — echo through the office without answering it. Lots of dealers were on lots of museum black lists until they came up with an object that inflamed the blind curatorial will to possess. Today there was no need for him to profess righteousness. Molenaar had invested in an expensive fish dinner across the pond from Parliament, with the Keeper of the Export List, to ensure that the de Gheyn stay off it.

'As you can see, I really would like to buy the painting, Lodewijk. But the final decision isn't mine, and you're going to have to convince two other people first. I've softened them up as best I could. At Restoration you're going to have to talk condition and price to my director. And I've set up an appointment for drinks at five o'clock with the man who will have to put up the money for the purchase, our board member Ernest

Wanamaker. He is interested in horses and history with a capital H. Two capital H's. One way or the other, we'll know by six whether the deal can be done.'

The painting they went to see in the conservation studio was a life-size profile portrait of a white stallion. It was not the kind of painting the Metropolitan would ordinarily be interested in. In Europe, it would hang in a historical museum rather than a picture gallery, with a long caption to make it more interesting. Altstad noted on the credit side that the Met had recently started writing long captions. The condition of the painting was a debit. It had spent its first century in a dank hallway in the palace of the Nassaus in Brussels, where armor would fall onto it and men with lances would bump into it. Once every year or two, it would be rubbed down with a dirty rag, pushing the surface dust into the widening cracks. Molenaar had not had the painting stripped of its patches and repairs, but Altstad had a good idea of the depressing sight that would greet the one who did. So did Auge and the restorer, who had undoubtedly scrutinized the wares under ultraviolet, infrared and raking light. But with Auge behind him, Altstad did not have to be too apologetic about condition.

The divisional director, Franklin Taft, was half Auge's age and seemingly twice his height. He was the top black official in the museum, an affirmative action appointee of the seventies who had worked his way from a token position to one of power by being more conservative than anyone else around. Taft was no more polite than he had to be. Actually, he was less polite than that. 'I don't mind telling you, Mr. Altstad, that I wouldn't spend a cent of our acquisitions budget on this white horse of yours — or is it a white elephant?' He made some clicking noises with his glottis which Altstad realized with horror were intended as laughter. 'But Auge here has gotten Mr. Wanamaker all hot about it, so I won't stand in your way. If I did I might be trampled, hehhehhehhehheh. So tell me, what is your asking price?'

'Eight hundred and fifty thousand dollars.'

'Tiens! For that money we could have a big, juicy, Suzanne

Valadon nude and the ladies would be off my back for a while. Can't we turn your painting into a Lady Godiva by a woman artist? Hehhehhehhehheh. It's not my money, but still I couldn't advise Mr. Wanamaker to pay that much. At least, not unless you contributed towards the restoration costs.'

'What do you mean?'

Taft picked up a clipboard from the restorer's desk.

'Your horse is painted on five warped oak panels flattened onto an ancient cradle. If the airlines knew what kind of tension that painting is under, they wouldn't have flown it over here. We are going to have to remove the cradle, and you know what that means. Fixing the surface — all nine and a half thousand precious square inches of it — detaching whatever laths let themselves be detached and then scraping, scratching, burning and biting off the rest. I'm glad I don't have to do it. If this were a Poussin — now, why did that example pop into my head?' (Auge returned Taft's sneering gaze blankly) 'we would rebuild the entire support. Seeing as it's only a de Gheyn, we'll flatten the panels with moisture and put the whole thing in a climate control box.

'Paint loss is over twenty percent, thanks to all those joins. The overpainting looks like it was done by some Dutch boy scout earning a merit badge for art . . .' Delighted with himself, Taft paused to improve on this bon mot. '. . . With fingers that had been stuck in the dike for too long. Hehhehhehhehheh. The craquelure is stuffed with filth and old inpainting. Extracting that will be like operating on a tumor covering half of someone's brain.' The director had the delicacy not to giggle. 'Getting this wreck in shape for the gallery is going to cost a lot. A whole lot. And it all comes off your price.'

There was no quarreling with the analysis. Altstad and Molenaar knew all of this — and worse — about the panel, and they had anticipated this part of the negotiations. Molenaar had decided not to spend the eighty thousand guilders it would have cost to repair the de Gheyn in The Hague. Since the museum was bound to find fault with the condition of the painting anyway, better let them blame it on time than on Molenaar. The only question was how much the Met would try to take off from the price. With restoration costs in New York running twice as high as in Holland, the job could cost them as much as eighty thousand dollars.

'I'd say, I'd say . . . a hundred and fifty thousand. Yes, one fifty should do the job. That leaves you with seven hundred for the painting, Mr. Altstad. Will that be all right?'

Altstad had the numbers in his head. Molenaar expected him to bring home one and a half million guilders. With the dollar at two-o-five, Taft's offer was sixty-five thousand guilders short. A little less than Altstad's commission of five percent. Altstad could already hear his great friend and mentor in Amsterdam explaining amicably why the shortfall had to come out of his commission. If he wanted to earn anything on this sale, he had to get it out of Taft, now. How would it be if they split the difference? Taft was overasking by seventy thousand dollars. Thirty-five would cover Molenaar's price. There was not much risk that the deal would run astrand on half of Taft's premium.

'I would be very happy to agree, Mr. Taft, but I'm afraid we really cannot accept that much of a cut. We have already ab-sorbed considerable out-of-pockets. Just packing and shipping the panel here put us to great expense, which you are being spared. Not to mention the risk, which is still ours. However, I do see your point about the cost of restoration. We are willing to go further than halfway towards your demand. Say seven hun-dred and thirty-five thousand dollars.'

Taft produced a thirty-five thousand dollar scowl. He didn't know how badly Wanamaker wanted his name on the label, to be immortalized as the donor of this big white Dutch mess. Wanamaker was new on the board of trustees, and Taft had not had dealings with him yet. He had a reputation as a non-stop, high-power worker, an omnivorous consumer of information, a charismatic leader of men, a merciless destroyer of anything and anyone between him and his goals — in short, the new standard image on the Street. Taft decided not to take a chance on being perceived by Wanamaker as an impediment. He glared at Altstad.

'If that is how it has to be, that is how it has to be. I will tell Mr. Wanamaker that eight-fifty is a fair price. Since we cannot bill you for the hundred and fifteen thousand dollar contribution towards restoration, I would appreciate it if you would provide sponsorship in that amount for our exhibition of portraiture at the court of Louis XV. Who knows, it might boost your reputation to share billing with the old Paris houses who have already become patrons.'

Altstad let the condescending remark stand. He had the feeling that none of the $115,000 would go to the restoration of the de Gheyn. Taft would charge that to Auge's budget, and use the sponsor money to pay for trips to Paris with the new curator of French painting. People said they were lovers.

'No problem, just let me know how to remit. We'll pay as soon as we cash Mr. Wanamaker's check. Assuming that Mr. Wanamaker decides to buy the painting for you.'

'That's entirely up to him. But I'll tell him we want it.'

3 / Manhattan, Monday afternoon

As Katy Eskenazi opened the door of her apartment, Altstad glided inside. Without saying anything, he embraced her and began kissing her intently, examining her face closely between kisses. They had been separated for a month, too long. Nothing he had to say could bypass his dumb need to make love to her. He went into a trance. He would have been satisfied to kiss her forever in the doorway, but somehow the door closed and they moved to her bedroom. He had no need for either of them to undress as long as he could go on holding her and kissing her. But they did undress. He went on kissing and feeling her, with no aim but to continue doing just that. Yet, they did move on, he did kiss and lick her until she came, he did enter her and, almost sadly, come inside her. There was nothing more he wanted from sex, nothing more he wanted from life. Yet his hands continued to pat and stroke her, even as he passed out with his lips on hers. It was always this way when they made love for the first time after a separation. He knew he had no right to expect it to happen, but it always did.

When he opened his eyes, he saw Katy sitting on the edge of the bed facing the window, looking away from him and down. Something was wrong. He didn't want to know about it yet. She would tell him when she had to. He sat up and drew her back to him, holding her head in his hands and smiling at her blessedly. He babbled about missing her, about wanting to be with her always, as if both of them did not know that he would be gone in an hour, not knowing when he would be back again. She told him about the exhibition she was working on. She did not smile, she was preoccupied with something Altstad did not want to hear.

Katy made lunch: fettucine alla panna with pasta fresca from a traiteur on First Avenue. Altstad had once told her he ate his way through graduate school happily on Goodman's egg noodles with Breakstone's cottage cheese. She tried to feed him just as soothingly on an updated version. He *was* soothed as they sat in her small kitchen, a former hall closet of a York Avenue mansion which was now split into fifteen studio apartments.

'Lodewijk, your letters are wonderful. You must be the perfect correspondent. And the most faithful. There's a fax from you every single morning when I wake up. I reread them in the street on my way to the subway and I live on them for the rest of the day. I know more about what you are doing than Emma Rae does about John. And they're married and living together *and* they work in the same building. I'm sure I get more love from you in the letters than she gets from him. When I get to the studio, I'm wet and sticky from you, and I'm that way most of the day.'

She had told him this before, and it thrilled Altstad. He played on it in his letters. Writing them excited him too, and so did Katy's letters to him. But this time there was something resentful in her tone. He was afraid of what was to come. Without her changing expression or seeming to notice it, tears started to run down her cheeks. 'I don't want you to write to me any more. I don't want to live with you in my head. You and I are creating a kind of half-fake love on paper. It's worse than a total fake, because it's made out of real pieces of ourselves, filled out with our imaginations. That is what I am in love with, and that is what you are in love with. It's even different for both of us. We are using each other to invent make-believe lovers. What's the good of that?'

As soon as Altstad caught on to the drift of Katy's complaint, he started thinking up rejoinders. He did not know what she meant by asking him to stop writing. Was this a way of saying that she had met someone else and wanted to break up with him? Or did she want more of him, more time together? Marriage? He felt sudden guilt at this reaction. Don't look for ulterior meanings, he said to himself, listen to her words, she's telling you something that's important to her. But he was in a panic at the thought he might lose her.

'It isn't the worst thing in the world. Every relationship has projection and fantasy, and the way we do it I think is just wonderful. Of course it's terrible when we don't see each other for a month, but in the meanwhile, we spend hours every day in each other's company, in our minds and in our feelings. I may be kidding myself about you a little, but no more than anyone else does about someone he's crazy in love with.'

When Katy smiled, Altstad relaxed a little. All was not lost. He even took a bite of the prune hamantasch he had brought for dessert from the Hungarian bakery between First and Second.

'I know that, Lodewijk. But it's not that simple. I don't know how to say this, or if I should say it.' She turned to him and took both his hands in hers. 'There is something strange about the way you write. Your letters are — they're too real. It's as if you're living off there in Holland or wherever you are with some other me you prefer to me. I didn't realize it until last week. We hadn't been apart for longer than twenty days before. Your letters always made me feel like a superior being, like Jacqueline Onassis or Georgia O'Keeffe or Madonna. I was nicer to people, out of pure noblesse oblige. I thought it was so sad for them that they were not as special as me. But last week I started to feel *in*ferior. I was on my way to the subway, acting like the image in your letter: I was the sexiest woman in New York, the best artist, with the best taste in clothes and jewelry and makeup, a perfect personality in a perfect body, and modest to boot. I was waiting for a light when a truck passed, with this gleaming metal finish. I saw myself wavering in space, getting tall and skinny, then short and fat, in a second. When the truck was gone, I was left with the reflection of myself in the mirror of your letter and the thought, held over from the truck: No, that's not me. And I realized that your picture of me was an even more grotesque distortion than the reflection in the truck. What made it worse is that I really believed your picture. No, I invented it. Those are all things about myself that I wanted to believe. If you hadn't come along, I would have pictured myself as the sexiest woman in New York and all the rest of those things anyway. But I wouldn't have believed it in the same way. You picked up on my picture of myself and turned it into a real image. Once I thought of this, I just collapsed. I was humiliated that I needed these ridiculous compliments.

'The worst thing is that my feelings toward you changed as well. You turned into a kind of demon, offering me the greatest gifts on earth, the things I really, really wanted, in exchange for my soul. I know this isn't fair to you. You were just respecting my own stupid insecurities. But from that moment you were less of a real person to me.'

Altstad knew what she meant, and knew she was right. He felt wicked writing those letters. Knowing how she would react, it was as if he were manipulating her feelings. The distance and time between stimulus and response gave him an extra thrill, like the slow pace of their lovemaking. But she was also right in saying that she had let him know, unspokenly, that she needed him to write those letters. He would have loved her just as much without writing them, or if he had sent her nothing more than yesterday's pages from his pocket diary. The unfairness was obvious, and she knew that too. There was nothing he could say. She was taking back responsibility for her co-authorship of the Katy Eskenazi they had conspired to create. He could only hope the move would not end in disaster for them.

'You have to promise not to write anymore, until I shake off that ghost we made.'

'Letters or no letters, Katy, I love you more than anything. I can't stand the idea that I might lose you. And only because I was writing too much.'

'I love you more than anything too, Lodewijk. And I wouldn't do anything deliberately to hurt you or to risk losing you. But we've put up this thing between me and the real world, and it's got to go. I don't know anymore what I am without it, so I can't even give you love that I know is real. That's all I want. How long are you in New York this time? Can you stay over tonight?'

'It's too bad, but I can't. There's an auction this evening that's important to me, and afterwards I have a re-auction with a bunch of dealers. How about tomorrow night?'

'Tomorrow I'm going to be in Dutch Kills putting the final touches on my stuff for the group show. I have no idea how long it's going to take, but when I'm finished I know I'll just want to creep home and collapse. Can you come out there in the late afternoon? I'd love to show you the stuff for the exhibition. You have to see it after dark, though.'

Mitchell Fleishig devoured the dessert wagon of the Rugby Room with his eyes.

'If there were a God who cared about mankind, we wouldn't have to choose between apple strudel and cheese cake.'

His lunch partner moaned softly without seeming to notice it.

'So get a hypnodietician, like me. Every Wednesday morning Dr. Kali trances me and gives me a micro-cassette with fourteen mindmeals. Did you notice I listened to a memo recorder when we sat down? It was Dr. Kali mindfeeding me. All I ate was a dozen tiny belons and crudities, but I feel like after six helpings from the Sunday brunch buffet at Mr. H. I shed a key a week for three months now. Another three months and I'm a welter-weight like eighteen again. Mindmeals cost more than food, but so what and anyway I start to think they taste better. You want I introduce you to Dr. Kali? She will help you make your peace with God.'

Now that Blackbeard mentioned it, Fleishig realized that the man across the table was thinner than he recalled. Somehow, though, he still looked pudgy. An eerie combination of a wraith and a fat man.

'If that's your newest meshuga'as, Ivo, enjoy it in good health is all I can say. But I still see the old Ivo surrounding the new one. Maybe the spectral aura you got from your last therapist isn't shrinking along with the rest of you.'

'Do you think so? That could be very dangerous. I never imagined such a thing could happen. If you're right, I may pop away from my aura and suffocate inside myself. Waiter, I change my mind. I take the mudcake with whipped buffalo milk.'

For five years, Fleishig had been courting Blackbeard, who

owned a small theater on the alley between Rodeo and Beverly Drive that Fleishig wanted to buy. But Blackbeard was not selling the place. Every other month from October to June, on the first Saturday and Sunday afternoons of the month, from five to seven, the California Crovenian Repertory Company performed nineteenth and twentieth-century classics of the Crovenian stage there. The customers filled the box office with their shopping bags from an afternoon in Beverly Hills, and took them with them again when they went out to dinner. Those ten afternoons a year were the highpoint of Crovenian cultural life on the west coast, and Blackbeard was solemnly proud to be part of it. He had the secret ambition of one day becoming the Minister of Culture of an independent Crovenia.

For the rest of the year, the hall was used for unscheduled screenings of fuckflicks, gashers and snuffers. Distributors from all over the world would let Blackbeard know what they were shopping for, and he would find them the newest products in their line. He also arranged for introductions to the actors and actresses, or rather to lookalikes whom no Japanese or Thai could tell from the lovely young things on the screen. The business, which grew out of the sale of orgone boxes, had made Blackbeard a rich man. It also provided him with the pleasure of coaching the lookalikes, whom he recruited in restaurants, barbershops and nail parlors.

To Fleishig, the Crovenia Building was the missing link in a hypersite, the Mother of All Malls. He didn't own any of it, but it was the concept that counted. The other buildings on the site were buyable for a price. Fleishig kept tabs on them from a distance. Only the Crovenia Building was a problem. Every few months, he dreamed blissfully of Blackbeard signing a contract. The paper would float into his hands. Without his having to grasp it, it stayed between his fingers as he turned around and exchanged it, with a faceless man behind a desk, for a check for $500,000,000.00. 'Half a bil,' the man said. It gave him the same feeling he used to have as a child, when he dreamed of finding nickels, dimes and quarters in the street and woke up with clenched fists. As he opened them, his euphoria would melt into tragic letdown.

Fleishig took Blackbeard out to lunch regularly to try to tempt him into selling. But Blackbeard was not interested in selling. His work kept him young, he said, and he had no wish to retire. His customers liked the location. The Crovenians felt that their literature belonged in an alleyway, and the film distributors appreciated the idea that anyone seeing them leaving their limos to duck into a back door would assume they were being shepherded discreetly into one of the world-class jewelry or clothing stores on the block. Beverly Hills was easy to reach from the San Fernando Valley, from the house where Blackbeard and his wife had been living since the children were small. As at every Blackbeard lunch, Fleishig again had to listen politely to the infuriatingly petty reasons which were keeping him from becoming the Donald Trump of the west coast. Today he had trouble paying attention.

The waiter brought a telephone to the table.

'Call for you, Mr. Fleishig.'

'Mitchell, it's Rodney. I got your fax, and I've just held an emergency meeting to discuss your problem. I'll get right to the point. We can't advance you anything on your collection.'

'You don't mean that, Rodney.'

'I did everything I could, but that's the upshot. I don't know if you've been following the market, but Old Masters are in free fall. Last week we tried to sell another LA collection: Brod Carruther's Italian paintings. We were laughed off the podium and he ended up owing us more in charges than he cleared from the bidding. He's been buying longer than you have, so your paintings have been on the market more recently than his. This is the worst possible moment to sell.'

'Listen to me, you mothersucker. When you were a junior curator you told me to buy those Utrecht pictures. I paid you good for advice, and that's what I got. Top price-quality ratio, you said, blind spot in the market's eye, money in the bank.

Now you're a fucking big shot at an auction house, you *are* the bank, and you tell me *this*?'

'That kind of talk is not going to get you anywhere.'

'It isn't? If I wasn't sitting in a full restaurant I'd really tell you something. Did the museum know what you were taking from me? And from Carruther, for that matter? We must have been fucking doubling your salary. What I'm asking you for has nothing to do with today's market. You don't have to sell now — you don't have to sell ever. All you've got to do is shake a little change out of those deep pockets. In a few months I'll take the art back. I'm calling in my notes, Rodney.'

'Whatever obligation I might have felt toward you for old times' sake went up in smoke about thirty seconds ago, Mitchell.'

'You fucking little mamser, you . . .' Click.

Fleishig had been talking louder than he thought. Voices at the other tables had subsided and Fleishig's end of the conversation was now on the grapevine. Mitchell Fleishig was a wounded beast.

'Well, Ivo, now you know I'm having trouble selling my art collection. You collect, too, don't you? Are you interested in some top goods at distress-sale prices?'

'What kind of goods?'

'Some of the most beautiful and technically proficient paintings from the Golden Age of Dutch painting.'

'Old paintings?'

Fleishig sensed that his common ground with Blackbeard was tilting downhill fast.

'Yes, very special ones.'

'I only like new paintings. My brother sends me every Christmas the best new paintings from a village near our home town where everybody learned to paint. They lost their farms, so they paint sheep and horses; they lost their church, so they paint angels and the Mother of God; their houses were knocked down and they were moved to crummy apartments, so they paint old-time scenes with crooked streets and peasants in costumes. They have no way of making a real living, so they all become artists. It brings the tears to our eyes, my wife and me. Last year's paintings we give away as Christmas gifts.'

'That's very heartwarming.'

'Yes, it is. Our hearts go very warm from art. But I hear from your voice that you are in trouble not just about art. I know lots about trouble. Most trouble is not so bad as it seems, and if you play by ear it stops being trouble after a while. But some trouble is really bad, and then you have to do something drastic. I can't tell you what it is, I don't want to know your trouble and you don't want me to. But you think about it yourself, and you will know what you have to do.'

'I'm sure those are wise words. Thank you.'

Across the room, a vice-president of the First American Bank of Beverly Hills was settling the bill for lunch. 'Tell me, waiter, who was the gentleman who took that phone call a few minutes ago?'

'His name is Mitchell Fleishig, sir.'

'Thank you.'

To his lunch companion, the vice-president muttered, 'Sounds familiar. I think Mr. Fleishig has an account with us. I'd better have a chat with his loan officer.'

'Gentlemen, we are going to dock in forty-five minutes. By then you will know my decision.'

Ernest Wanamaker's yacht cast off from a pier in the 79th Street Marina, surged into the stale pink mist of a premature Hudson River twilight, and headed north with Wanamaker, Lodewijk Altstad and Frederick Auge on board. From a velvet box in his attaché case, Wanamaker removed a silver flask and three silver shot glasses. He poured them full and passed them around.

'Twenty-five-year old single malt from my distillery in Craghbourne. To your health. Mr. Altstad, tell me about the Jack O'Gain.'

Say what you like about the Institute, thought Altstad. After four years of presenting seminar papers to scornful professors and contentious peers, you could roust him out of bed, fly him halfway around the world, shake up his love life, take him into the middle of a polluted river, force whisky down his throat, and he could still talk first-class art history without missing a stroke.

'The Battle of Nieuwpoort, Mr. Wanamaker, was a legendary incident in the Dutch struggle for independence from Spain. What Iwo Jima was in the Pacific War, was Nieuwpoort in the Eighty-Year War.' ('Dutch inversion,' he thought. 'You're tired. Watch it.' He redoubled his concentration and went on.) 'And it became legendary partly because of a work of art with an appealing image, an image that became iconic and grew more significant than the action of the battle or its strictly military importance. Again, like Iwo Jima.'

Wanamaker, taking a sip of whisky with his right hand, held out his left in a gesture commanding silence and attention. He held his hand out until he had swallowed, then lowered it to

Altstad's knee, leaned towards him and looked him in the eye penetratingly. He spoke confidentially yet portentously, as if letting Altstad in on the deeper meaning of his own words.

'What you're saying is very interesting. What you're saying is the main principle I always try to inculcate in my people. What you're saying . . . is . . . that perCEPtion is everything. PerCEPtion . . . is . . . EVerything.'

This was not what Altstad was saying. He contained himself, took a deep breath, returned Wanamaker's gaze and repeated to himself Mentor Wim Molenaar's Lesson Number One: never contradict or correct the customer; his misconceptions are your best friends. The occasion on which he learned this expensive lesson — when he won an argument with and thereby lost a sale to the curator of Dutch and Flemish paintings in Berlin — came back to him in all its painfulness. He nodded and put on a frown of intense intellectual effort.

'That's a very profound thought. Your staff is fortunate to have such a powerful guideline to go by.'

'I only wish they understood it as well you do, Mr. Altstad. But please, I interrupted you. Go on with your presentation.'

With the receding midtown skyline and the darkening Jersey Palisades to distract him and the unaccustomed sensation of hurtling over the water by night to unsettle him, Altstad went on.

'The commander on the Dutch side was Maurits of Orange-Nassau, the stadholder. He was the son of William the Silent, whom the Dutch worshipped as a martyr and the Father of His Country. Maurits did not have the same appeal as his father. He was a fighting man with a court consisting largely of German mercenaries. The Eighty Years War was his bread and butter, and he was not inclined to stop it. Around 1600, peace talk was in the air. The battle of Nieuwpoort, for Maurits, was just as much a provocation against the peace faction in Holland as an attack against the Spanish in the southern Netherlands. It was very important for him to win. Or at least not to lose.

'His opposite number was the Hapsburg Archduke Albert,

son of the late Emperor Maximilian II and the new bridegroom of Archduchess Isabella, the daughter of the late Philip II of Spain. Two years earlier, in the year of his death, Philip had given the southern Netherlands to his daughter. Albert and Isabella were having a hard time holding up their end of the battle against the rebelling northern provinces. Their troops were not getting paid regularly, and mutiny was threatened. To rally his army for Nieuwpoort, Albert had to pawn Isabella's jewels. It was important for him to win as well.

'Two German princes, one running the northern Netherlands and the other the southern Netherlands, for the Spanish. Today that kind of thing only happens in multi-national corporations. Countries only get ruled by local talent. I wonder what that means.'

Altstad was giving Wanamaker an opening, expecting to be treated to a philosophy of nations and companies and human resources. He looked at him for a sign, and saw to his astonishment that Wanamaker had cut off his end of eye contact. The banker's eyes were open, but he had rolled his eyeballs out of sight. He was staring into the insides of his eyelids. Was he seeing anything? Was he awake? Altstad looked to Auge for guidance, but his forehead was resting against the window, his eyes, open or shut, turned away. In mild panic, unsure whether anyone was listening to him, Altstad went on.

'Maurits was better at siege warfare than the kind of pitched battle that took shape at Nieuwpoort. But he had luck that day. They were fighting on the coast, and as the battle progressed, the tide was going out. Maurits managed to get his artillery onto the hard sand, with his cavalry in the dunes. Albert's army was bogged down in the loose sand, and the Dutch killed or captured half his men as the others retreated to terra firma. At that point, Maurits decided to proclaim himself the glorious winner and call it a day.

'During the battle, Maurits' young cousin Lodewijk Günther captured a famous white stallion that had been given to Albert by the king of Spain. Lodewijk Günther presented it to Maurits, and it became a symbol of the victory. Three years later, the symbol came in handy. The Spanish had regrouped, and their crack general Ambrogio Spinola was laying siege to the Dutch harbor town of Oostende, exactly the situation that the Battle of Nieuwpoort was supposed to prevent. At this point, Maurits commissioned a life-size portrait of Albert's horse. Using art to pump up the status of the victory at Nieuwpoort as a way of counteracting the threatened loss of Oostende. In your terms, Mr. Wanamaker, Maurits was massaging the world's perception of the battle.

'The choice of the painter was part of the perceptual manipulation. Maurits gave the commission to a brilliant artist named Jacques de Gheyn the Second. De Gheyn had recently designed and engraved the manual of arms for Maurits, a complete visual course of instruction in the use of the musket. Those engravings were so valuable for training that they gave the army of the States General a strategic edge. Maurits prohibited their publication for ten years, treating them like a military secret. But the prints had already established their legendary reputation, and de Gheyn along with them. His name on the portrait of the horse reinforced the image of Maurits as the smartest and most successful condottiere in Europe.'

If Wanamaker and Auge were not asleep, there was no way Altstad could tell. Was anyone listening to him? The helmeted skipper certainly wasn't. He probably did not even hear the engine as well as Altstad did. 'If a tree falls in a lonely forest, does it make a sound?' Altstad asked himself. 'Am I making sounds? Am I still real?' He acted on the assumption that he was, not out of conviction but because he was afraid to test the alternative.

'The painting was completed in 1603. A young groom is leading the horse to the left, in an empty stable. Daringly enough, that's all, except for the inscription above the horse. It's a Latin chronogram — a poem in which the numeral letters I, V, X, L, C and M add up to a year, in this case the year 1600. The poem was by a young genius at the University of Leiden, Hugo Grotius, who was to become the father of international law. The poem says 'The Spanish earth brought it forth and gave it to the Austrian; Flanders presented it to the conqueror Maurits.' The horse is presented as a symbol of the push and pull between great nations, with the leader of the Dutch rebels coming out on top of the imperial forces.

'Maurits was pleased with the painting, but de Gheyn, perhaps unwisely, went on record saying that he wasn't. In 1604, de Gheyn's friend Carel van Mander published his book on the painters of the Netherlands, which is still our standard source. His life of de Gheyn contains information that could not have come from anyone but the painter himself. Van Mander wrote that de Gheyn was always trying to improve himself. In flower painting, he reached his top around the turn of the century, when he sold a large still-life — an improved version of a smaller painting — and an album of drawings to Emperor Rudolph II. Rudolph was the older brother of Archduke Albert, so in commissioning de Gheyn to paint Albert's captured stallion, Maurits was also recruiting a painter away from the Hapsburgs. The commission was a quantum leap for de Gheyn, from the miniature to the monumental. This was the kind of opportunity he had been waiting for. But when it was finished, he told van Mander, he wasn't satisfied, even if his patron was. The painting is now in the Rijksmuseum in Amsterdam. A canvas, in terrible condition. Some blame the damage on the Rijksmuseum restorers, but I don't agree.

'After a three-year-siege, the Dutch lost Oostende, and the war went into stalemate. In 1609, the peace party was able to finesse a truce for twelve years. For the first time in a generation, open commerce between the northern and southern Netherlands was possible. Among the first entrepreneurs to take advantage of the situation were artists on both sides of the line. The artistic community of the north consisted largely of immigrants from the south. Jacques de Gheyn was typical: he was born in Antwerp. Once the truce was in effect, he started looking for ways of branching out into his native territory.

'That much is on the books. What I am about to tell you is

not. It is a new theory, surmised from the existence of the newly-discovered painting we're talking about.'

They were under the Tappan Zee Bridge when Altstad got to the heart of his story. Wanamaker turned in his chair, rolled his eyes down to fix Altstad with his gaze, then rolled them back up again. Altstad soldiered on.

'At de Gheyn's level, there was no reason for him not to aim for top patronage in the south. The biggest market was in Antwerp, where rich merchants ordered commissions for their own town and country houses and for churches. But the merchants tended to spend their money on artists whose standing was validated by the court of the archdukes. That was the place to start, but the archdukes were unapproachable sorts, certainly for a Protestant emigrant. You needed a highly-placed middleman to get to them. De Gheyn thought he knew one: a Nassau prince, an older half-brother of Maurits, at the heart of the archducal court. This was the strange Philips Willem, who had been raised in Spain as an honored hostage while his father and brothers were fighting Spanish domination of the Netherlands. In fact, Philips Willem was actually at the Battle of Nieuwpoort, although he did not fight that day.

'De Gheyn had the dubious inspiration of using the horse as a re-entry device. He got permission from Maurits to make a full-size copy of the portrait. He provided it with a different inscription, praising Albert as the champion of the arts of peace. The idea was to have Philips Willem present it to Archduke Albert, while introducing the painter. It isn't hard to invent reasons why this didn't work. Be that as it may, the painting stayed in the Nassau Palace in Brussels for more than two hundred years. No one was sure who it belonged to — the painter, the archdukes or the house of Nassau, the heirs to Philips Willem's estate after his death in 1618. The painting is on panel, and on the whole is in better shape than the canvas in the Rijksmuseum. If de Gheyn was as good as his word to van Mander, it is also an improved version, which I would be prepared to argue. But I will leave it up to Dr. Auge to make that case in the article he will be writing on the painting for the museum bulletin if the sale goes through.

'The painting has never been on the market and has never been published. Thanks to the Congress of Vienna, the house of Orange-Nassau made it back to Brussels in 1815 as kings of a united northern and southern Netherlands. Willem I, who was called the businessman-king, was a great backer of commercial enterprise — preferably with symbolic rather than financial means — and the painting came in handy for him. When one of his new men opened an express coach service between Brussels and The Hague in 1820, Willem gave him the painting in token of his royal esteem. Later he made him postmaster-general. The descendants of that man, Baron Achterhoofd, are the first sellers of the painting since 1609.'

That was Altstad's spiel. This is what Molenaar was paying him five percent for. The quality of the art history was not what really mattered. If Molenaar were selling the painting, there would have been less history and more rhapsodizing about the modelling and the color. That worked just as well if not better. What Molenaar needed Altstad for were his American manners and clothing and pronunciation. His sleek build and curly black hair and the fun smile that even between smiles seemed to dwell in his dimple as a pledge of good humor.

To curators and collectors who knew Dutch art, Willem Molenaar was a legend. Without having to admit it to themselves, they knew that they were better off trusting his judgment than their own. But buying decisions were increasingly influenced by people outside the art world, like trustees, sponsors, politicians. In dealing with them, Molenaar's appearance and personality were a drawback. He dressed and talked like a floorwalker in a chain store, the kind of person who would be removed from someone like Wanamaker by three levels of command. His English was comprehensible to the interested listener, but it was disastrously reminiscent of the comic greenhorn from a thirties movie. An American meeting him for the first time would be unable to take him seriously. Altstad was more like one of the smart young graduates that a Wanamaker had around him all the time and whom he liked to impress. It was a credit to Molenaar's insight and self-knowledge that he did not take any of this personally, but simply used Altstad in American situations where it would help to make a sale.

Wanamaker had started to stir when the engine was cut back to half speed. As the yacht twirled for its reverse approach to the pier on his estate below Croton, Wanamaker's eyeballs reappeared.

'That is an astonishing coincidence, Mr. Altstad. My ancestor John Wanamaker was postmaster-general under our President Benjamin Harrison. The U.S. Post Office must still have been using horses back then. I hadn't thought of that before. We could do a brochure on the donation, with pictures of that baron of yours and my ancestor. Mr. Taft tells me the painting is worth the $850,000 you are asking. Here is my card, Mr. Altstad. Please make out the invoice to The Wanamaker Family Trust at this address.'

The mate jumped onto the pier and pulled the yacht in.

'You are very welcome to join Dr. Auge and me for a drink in the house, but if you have to be in the city by seven I recommend that you sail straight back. It was a pleasure meeting you. I hope to see you again at the presentation. Good evening.'

'Lot 34. Flemish school.'

On the screen an image appeared of the painting that was being held up to the well-filled hall of Old York Auctioneers. The audience reacted to the representation with gasps, giggles and wisecracks. What they saw was a large, malevolent beaked creature covered with green and red feathers, glaring over one wing toward a billow of toxic-looking smoke on the right.

The auctioneer, whose lank hair was too gray and too sparse for a man not yet forty, was slouched back in his chair, in a pose straddling the not too fine line between desultoriness and body-language putdown. He lisped the bids in a tone to match.

'What am I bid for our fine feathered friend? The opening bid is six thousand dollars in my book.'

The lot was estimated at six to eight thousand dollars. Altstad knew that a ring of five dealers in Dutch and Flemish paintings had agreed to go one bid above double the high estimate. For inconspicuous lots at minor sales, at which they were likely to be the only serious bidders, the participants in the ring were able to keep the hammer price down by not bidding against each other. After the sale they would re-auction the goods among themselves. All the members of the ring shared in the difference between the hammer price and the amount paid by the successful bidder. This money would otherwise go to the seller. Altstad knew that a ring was bidding on lot 34 because Willem Molenaar was in it, and he was standing in for Molenaar. Speelberg was assigned by the other ring members to do their bidding.

'Six thousand here. Are we done?'

Speelberg caught the auctioneer's eye and nodded.

'Seven thousand up front. Anyone else?'

The auction house was not supposed to know there was a

ring. When dealers joined up to bid on a lot they were required to advise the house in advance that they were doing so. Unregistered rings were invisible to the seller and the audience, but not to the house. They were better acquainted than anyone with the dealers in Dutch and Flemish paintings, and when there was only one bidder from the trade on an interesting painting, he had to be representing a ring. Old York was expected to crack down on such illegal conspiracies, but if there is anything an auction house hates, it is playing policeman.

The house knew that if the ring was bidding, it was not going to stop at the estimate. It would certainly go to twice the average of the high and low estimates — fifteen thousand dollars for this lot. The auctioneer made a show of consulting some papers at his desk and came up with a write-in bid that may or may not have existed.

'Eight thousand in my book.'

In the front of the hall was a row of desks manned by auction house staff with marked catalogues and telephones. The auctioneer looked meaningfully at the young man closest to him. The young man looked meaningfully back.

'Nine thousand to my right.'

The auctioneer used the young man as a ventriloquist's dummy to get the bidding up to fourteen thousand dollars, then looked back at Speelberg, who nodded.

'Sixteen thousand.'

The figures succeeded each other at the top line of a board facing the audience, with the equivalent in German marks, Italian lire, Swiss and French franks, and Japanese yen beneath.

The auctioneer, confident that he had squeezed the ring for what it was worth, embarked on his quick knock-down routine in the accelerated mode.

A young woman colleague of his, the horn of a telephone wedged to her ear while she fumbled with her copy of the catalogue, squealed, 'No. Hold on a minute' and talked into the phone while the auctioneer picked up the cup of coffee on his lectern.

'I have a bid on the line,' she finally said.

The auctioneer looked at her quizzically, showing interest for the first time since the sale had started twenty minutes earlier.

'Eighteen thousand on the phone,' he announced.

Speelberg quickly made another bid for the ring.

'Twenty thousand in front of me.' He looked at the woman, who raised her pencil in the air.

'Twenty-two on the phone. Twenty-two.'

Smiling now, he returned his gaze to the dealer in the front row. Speelberg fidgeted. Twenty thousand dollars was a watershed bid. Even though he was now above twice the upper limit plus one bid, he knew the ring would not expect him to stop at twenty thou. He nodded peremptorily.

'And twenty-four.'

The pencil went up again.

'Twenty-six. Twenty-six on the phone. Twenty-six thousand dollars.'

Next to the young lady on the telephone was a middle-aged man seated at a desk like hers, gazing blandly into the hall. In fact, throughout the bidding on this lot Philip Pleasure had been seeing no one but Altstad, who now looked him straight in the eye and raised his catalogue to his cheek. Pleasure turned commandingly to the desk and nodded.

'Twenty-eight thousand dollars.' The auctioneer was now sitting straight up in his chair. *Two* customers topping the ring on an unsigned, unattributed painting of a feathered monster? There were people out there who thought they knew more about the painting than Old York or the consignor. Obviously, the house had missed a trick. But then again, so had the ring.

There was a brief consultation on the telephone, and the young woman bid once more.

'Thirty thousand.'

Alstad was no less curious than the auctioneer to know who was on the phone. From his seat in the third row he began looking right and left for clues without moving his head. He had to keep his copy of the catalogue against his right cheek where it could be seen. Until he lowered it, Pleasure would keep bidding for him. Alstad was going against a ring in which he was involved, but, he told himself hypocritically, he wasn't really in it, was he? Molenaar was. Altstad only happened to know what the ring was up to.

'Thirty thousand dollars on the phone.' The auctioneer called it out to the hall, looking as if he expected the onlookers to be as nonplussed as he was. They were starting to buzz the way they did when any lot goes to a multiple of its high estimate, but none of them knew what made the bidding on lot 34 different. No one, at least, but Altstad and Speelberg, the only other dealer from the ring at the sale. From where he sat, Altstad could see the back of Speelberg's head in his invariable seat in the front row, on the aisle to the right. He wondered whether Speelberg was the president of his congregation.

'Thirty-three thousand dollars.' The bid was from Pleasure, who was enjoying himself keenly, as those could tell who were unfortunate enough to know the signs.

Altstad, glued to his catalogue and to Philip Pleasure, noticed motion up front. Speelberg was standing up and turning around to study the hall fiercely. It was Speelberg! Speelberg was bidding outside the ring. It was his bid on the phone. He could not give new instructions, and was in danger of losing a painting he thought he had in his pocket. He was looking to see if anyone from the ring was in the room. If not, he could still get someone to bid against Pleasure for him. Altstad poked his head up brightly and smiled at his colleague. Speelberg froze as his eyes met Altstad's. He sat down slowly.

'Thirty-six thousand.' This was Speelberg's last bid, Altstad thought. One bid above four times the high estimate. A failsafe, knockout, pre-emptive bid, especially for someone who knew that the ring was stopping halfway. It was like setting your VCR for four hours to tape a one-hour program. But Speelberg had run out of tape. Pleasure gave the auctioneer a grinning Yes and poised a pen above lot 34 in his catalogue.

'Forty thousand dollars.' The girl's hand did not go up again.

She nodded No at the auctioneer. Speelberg, sitting not ten feet away from her, grunted loudly. The auctioneer's expression displayed a slight glimmer. He now knew half the riddle.

'Forty thousand. Fair warning at forty thousand dollars.' He looked at Speelberg who grunted again, gnashed his teeth and lowered his head. 'Down it goes at forty thousand. To Philip's commission. Thank you both.' The gavel sounded, and the entry was duly made.

'Lot 35.'

For almost three hours, Altstad's commission of $36,750 on the sale of the de Gheyn had been burning a hole in his pocket. He could relax now. With the buyer's premium of ten percent, he was again solidly in the red. He was also more excited about his future than at any time since he got his fellowship to graduate school.

After the auction, Altstad wrote a check post-dated by two weeks to Old York, took his painting home and strolled downtown to Lilydale's gallery on East 57th Street. By 11:30, all the dealers in the ring had joined him. Besides Altstad, Lilydale and Speelberg, there was the Dutchman Karel Vingerling and the American Arthur van Doorn. The traditional crock of old Bols *jenever* came out of the refrigerator. None of them drank it on any other occasion, but they would not have wanted to defy fortune by switching to young *jenever*, as everyone in Holland did in the seventies. Although the ring was put together on an ad hoc basis per auction, and often had completely different participants, it was a venerable institution.

The business of the evening was to re-auction the painting they had bought at the sale. It was a poor night for the conspirators. Of the five lots on which they had bid, only one was knocked down to them, a low-life tavern scene by Cornelis Bega. The painting had gone to Speelberg for $45,000. Retail, you might get as much as $125,000 for it. Altstad, sitting in for Molenaar, stood to get the same five percent as for the sale of the de Gheyn, although he was acting on exact instructions.

'Rokin rules, gentlemen?' With the wry reference to the classic Amsterdam address for picture dealers, Lilydale was proposing that they use a Dutch knockout system for dividing the difference between what the ring had paid to the auction house and the amount the Bega was going to fetch at their re-auction. No one objected. Lilydale distributed identical pieces of paper and envelopes. Each of the dealers wrote down his name and an amount on the paper, put it in the envelope and gave it back to Lilydale. He opened them one by one.

'Speelberg 65,000. Lilydale 55,000. Molenaar 67,500. Vingerling 50,000. Van Doorn Buy at any price. It's yours, Arthur. Here's the pick-up slip.'

Lilydale took out a pocket calculator.

'Okay, let's see who gets what. Hammered down at $45,000, ten percent premium, that's forty-nine five for Old York. Karel, you get a fifth of the $50,000 you bid, is ten. I take that ten plus a quarter of the difference between my fifty-five and your fifty, gives me eleven two fifty. Irving,' he said, turning to Speelberg, 'you get $11,250 plus a third of the difference between your bid and mine. $14,583. Not bad. And Willem gets that and half of the small increment. Let's see . . . $15,813. Arthur, the Bega costs you $101,146. Here are the chits. I hope you have a customer, and I hope everybody is happy. Everybody except Old York, that is, and whoever was foolish enough to consign the painting to them for sale. Next time they'll know better. Some people are too greedy for their own good.'

Under the circumstances, Arthur van Doorn was moderately content. He was taking a big chance putting a blank check into the hat. If Speelberg had known that van Doorn had a customer for the painting, he might have put in a bid of a hundred thousand and earned more out of the transaction, with no risk, than the buyer. He could even have bid a hundred and fifty, and forced the buyer into loss. Speelberg had done this in the past, when a little birdie had told him that another of the dealers in a ring was going to put in a Buy bid.

Happiest of all, though he didn't know it yet, was the absent Willem Molenaar, pocketing fifteen thousand dollars for not bidding at an auction he didn't attend on a painting he didn't want. Altstad was satisfied to have cleared his airfare for the trip.

'Not much of a night,' Lilydale said to no one in particular. 'Except for the bidding on that monster. Anybody have an idea who bought it?' He looked searchingly at Speelberg.

Altstad delayed long enough to give Speelberg the chance to say something if he wanted to. When the silence was just right, he broke it.

'I did.'

They all turned to him in amazement. Lilydale was beside himself. '*You* did? And you say it just like that? What the fuck are you doing here? What the fuck do you think we all are doing here? You knew that we bid on that painting.'

'What I'm doing here, Mr. Lilydale, is running an errand for Willem Molenaar. Otherwise I have nothing to do with what is going on here, or with anybody else's bidding at the auction. As far as lot 34 is concerned, I bought it on my own account. Molenaar doesn't even know I was interested in it.'

Lilydale was fuming, looking for words. He slowed down.

'To us, tonight, you *are* Molenaar. As far as we are concerned, you are him. You are one of us. And one of us does not bid privately against the rest of us. That is what this is all about. Our business is based on confidence, and you' (the words 'and Molenaar' formed in his throat, but he swallowed them; tomorrow was another day) 'you betrayed that confidence.'

Altstad was expecting this outburst.

'I'm sorry if you feel that way. But I was not aware that I had been taken into your confidence. None of you invited me into this ring or any other. I was just executing Molenaar's instructions, which concerned only the knockout. At the sale, I was on my own. I'm sure Willem would back me up and would resent what you are implying. And anyway, I did not disadvantage you at the sale. Don't forget, the ring was not the underbidder. You wouldn't have gotten the painting even if I had not bid.' Altstad shifted his gaze between Lilydale and Speelberg.

Lilydale looked around the room. Van Doorn and Vingerling had 'He has a point' written all over their faces. They were not going to risk a fight with Molenaar. They earned some of their best money on commissions from Molenaar, who always knew before they did when a top-line painting was in play. It was Speelberg who spoke.

'I say, let's be reasonable. We had no deal with the kid, so it would not be right to penalize him. Let's give him a chance to show he's a mensch by cutting us in when he sells this painting. If he does, I for one would be in favor of putting him on the short list. This will also keep him from becoming a nuisance to us, like this evening.'

Altstad was impressed. While giving in, Speelberg was finessing Altstad out of a chunk of money. If he did not accuse Speelberg now of having bid against the ring, he would forever have to hold his peace. Not only could he not prove it, but he had nothing to gain by trying if he wanted to keep dealing in Dutch paintings.

Lilydale decided to let himself be assuaged. 'Do all of you go along with that?' They did. 'Do you, Mr. Altstad?'

'How much of a cut do you expect on the sale of the painting I bought tonight?'

'You're a young man, just beginning, you don't have much money, and we don't want to make things difficult for you. We're also not in the habit of telling each other for how much we sell paintings. The hammer price was $40,000? Let's say you owe each of us here $5,000, to be paid when you sell this painting. Whether you pay Molenaar or not we'll leave up to the two of you. You tell him what happened. And from now on you confer with us before any important Dutch or Flemish auction in New York, London or Amsterdam. We will not put up with a repetition of tonight.'

'*Akkoord*,' Altstad said in the Dutch word for resigned agreement. They all knew it.

Lilydale knocked back his drink and poured another. He looked hard at Altstad.

'I must admit that I am astonished that you are willing to put down sixty-five, seventy thousand dollars for that painting. What do you know about it that we don't know?'

'I have an idea that it's by Jan Steen.'

Speelberg camouflaged his grunt by choking over a sip of *jenever*. Lilydale patted him on the back. 'So you are as surprised as the rest of us, Irving. Do you believe him?'

'He's a smart kid. What he says I take seriously.'

When he arrived home, a yard-long fax was curled up on his rug. It was the galleys of his article in the *Kensington*. He looked it over briefly and then sent a fax of his own.

TELEFAX MESSAGE
from Lodewijk Altstad, New York, for:

HENRY WALKER
Reynolds Museum of Art, Houston, Texas

Pages (including this sheet): 18

Our fax: +1 (212) 875-4909
Our phone: +1 (212) 875-2778

Dear Mr. Walker,

I have a painting on offer in which you may be interested. It seems to be the missing left half of the Jan Steen *Bridal Pair* which the Reynolds acquired four years ago. It depicts a monster, which identifies the subject definitively as *The Wedding Night of Sarah and Tobias*. Attached are the proofs of a forthcoming article in the *Kensington Journal* with all the arguments.

If you would like to see the painting, please let me know at your earliest convenience. I can be reached at this fax for the next twenty-four hours.

With best wishes, yours sincerely,

In bed, Altstad could not keep himself from making one telephone call. He dialed London.

'Rich here.'

'Gordon,' Altstad said in his best New York accent. Gawd'n. 'Irving, did we get the Steen?'

Altstad smiled blissfully, hung up, and fell contentedly asleep.

Fleishig never stole more than one hand a night, two at the most. There were limits on what you could get away with if you wanted to stay in the game, and his Monday night poker game mattered to him. It was a game in which he could tip the odds.

If they were not playing at his house tonight he would have begged off. But he could not afford to demonstrate that much weakness to the table: the show-business money manager Lavin, the tax lawyer Ridley, the deputy mayor Loomer and the TV producer Gunhouse. Tonight they were six. A visiting fireman was sitting in: Fleishig's cousin Sheldon.

'Gentlemen, may I introduce Mr. Sheldon Fletcher. He is in the first place a dedicated poker player from Coral Gables, Florida, and in the second place my cousin. Sheldon and his wife are on their way to Hawaii for a couple of weeks. She's out with Beatrice, so I invited him over for our game. Is that all right with everyone?'

'Better now than on his way back. This way we get a crack at breaking him before his wife does.'

'Are you kidding? A guy with Ralph Lauren written all over him? He can handle her.'

'I hope we can handle him. Not much chance if he's got the luck of the Fleishigs.'

In the first hand, while everyone was still piling their chips and moving their drinks and settling into their chairs, Fleishig nicked the king of diamonds with his thumbnail. Every week he marked the first ace or face card he was dealt and then threw in the hand. This lowered the chance that his stolen pots resembled each other and covered him if anyone noticed the nick. No one else had held the card before him and no one knew he had had it.

Fleishig wondered whether Sheldon would catch on. They had played cards often enough since they were kids together in Brownsville. Poker became a family ritual in the fifties and had remained one. But he had never had to mark cards to win from the family. They used old decks which he could read like a book after a few hands.

There was a nervous mood at the table. Ridley was doing all the betting in one hand of draw poker after another. The others would stay in for the draw and then throw in their cards in self-disgust. Ridley kept raking in the meager results without anyone seeing what he was holding. Lavin was getting worked up; he tried to buy a pot from Ridley after drawing one card. But his raises lacked conviction, and no one was surprised that he turned out to be holding four hearts and a spade. Ridley won with a high pair, which left the table in doubt as to what he was really betting on. Lavin tried again to push Ridley out of a pot by raising, more decidedly, on two pairs. But now Ridley had three of a kind.

Only Fletcher seemed relaxed. When he was dealing for the second time he eased the pace of the game by shuffling slowly and then stopping with a sudden smile.

'You know, it must be a good forty-five years since Mitchell and I first played cards. We used to sneak out of the synagogue during the sermon and play go-fish in the basement. Later we played pinochle with the big kids.'

He changed the game to seven-card stud, which cut the tension. The banter and the drinking picked up.

When Loomer left the table for the toilet, Fletcher told another story. 'My earliest memory of Mitchell. Sutter Avenue, Brownsville. Around 1940. We're visiting Mitchell's family. It must be Saturday afternoon, because their grocery store, on the ground floor, is closed. I go to the window. Mitchell is playing on the sidewalk with a kid called Christopher. Christopher is taunting him. Holding a baseball glove on a bat up over his head where Mitchell can't get to it. Must be Mitchell's glove. I hear Christopher chanting "Mitch, Mitch, is a bitch. Mitch, Mitch, is a bitch." Mitchell is furious, frustrated as hell. "Christopher, Christopher . . .", he chants back. "Christopher, Christopher . . ." What rhymes with Christopher? Nothing. What does Mitchell do? In a fit of desperate inspiration he breaks the rules. Of poetry. And he breaks them good. "Christopher, Christopher," he shouts. "Christopher, Christopher is a . . . rattlesnake fuck." '

Great, Fleishig thought. What's he going to tell next? How I got expelled from business school? About the putz dean who accused me of hiring the goon who gunwhipped him? That I knocked up sweet Beatrice and married her for the money she turned out not to have? About the stillborn little boy? Why doesn't he tell how he got into the pants of a widow who did have money? Maybe I will.

Fleishig's hand didn't come up until one-thirty in the morning. He was dealing jacks or better. On the deal he got four cards to an inside straight. The missing card was a king, and the king of diamonds hadn't gone out yet. Ridley opened with two hundred dollars and Fleishig raised two. Everyone stayed in. Lavin was sitting to Fleishig's left. He asked for three cards. When Fleishig had dealt them his thumb felt the nick on the lower edge of the top card. He was pattering as always, to camouflage the click when it came. He was good enough to deal the second card from the top so no one could see it, but not good enough to do it without making a sound.

'AAAND . . . two cards for the visitor. Got the fourth ace, Sheldon? What'll YOU have, Ridley? One? Maybe this time it's a heart. "You gotta have heart," ' he sang the show tune as he dealt. When his own turn came he put one card on the table and helped himself to the king of diamonds off the top of the deck.

Fleishig started the second round of betting with five hundred dollars. Lavin dropped, Fletcher called and Ridley demonstratively raised a thousand. It looked so much like another of his four-flush bluffs that Loomer and Gunhouse called. Fleishig hadn't had this big a pot in months. On his regular game, which kept strictly to the book, he broke even. The one stolen hand is what kept him ahead of the game. An average of two thousand a week, week in week out. Tonight he could rake in a good eight thou.

'That'll be two to stay, gents,' Fleishig pronounced ceremoniously. He was now silent. Fletcher and Ridley called, Loomer and Gunhouse folded.

'Straight to the ace.' Fleishig laid his cards on the table. Ridley began to howl and groan.

'Look at that. Mine is to the queen. No more showdowns against Mitchell for me. I learned my lesson. Next time I'll drop with anything less than four aces.'

Mitchell was reaching for the pot when Sheldon cleared his throat.

'One second, cos.'

Sheldon flipped over his hand to show three nines and two fours. Fleishig felt a cramp in his gut.

'Why didn't you bet them?' He could not keep the reproach out of his strained voice. His own cousin, putting him a month behind the game.

Fletcher said nothing. He smiled apologetically and raked in the chips.

When two o'clock struck on the mantelpiece clock Fleishig announced, as the host did every week at that time, that the game would end after the current round. By two-fifteen everyone was out of the house and Fleishig was alone in the living room with Fletcher.

'Sheldon, can I ask you something important in confidence?'

Fletcher, who knew perfectly well what was coming and what his answer would be, managed without difficulty to look surprised and concerned.

'Of course.' He leaned forward and looked at Fleishig with appropriate seriousness.

'At this particular moment I have run into a kind of crisis. It's not business. I am in like the second echelon of major players in the projects market out here. And Los Angeles is not about to go away. We have fantastic prospects, and I'm in the center of where it's happening.'

'I don't doubt that. I'm proud as hell of you for having gotten there all on your own.'

'Well, that has its downside. When you start without capital you basically work with other people's money. They earn a lot on it, but it makes you vulnerable during the dips. And I don't have to tell you that we're in a dip. One of my partners is getting panicky — without reason, mind you — and wants to pull out. It's not all that much money, in the low seven figures, but at this point in time it would force me to sell some terrific holdings very disadvantageously. What I was wondering was whether you could see fit to pick up the slack for half a year or so. There's no risk, and I would cut you in on some fabulous action.'

'God, how I wish I could. But I don't have any money of my own. It's all Ethel's; I just get an allowance. And Ethel doesn't have that kind of cash either. Her capital is parked with Lazard Frères; they run the portfolio on their own discretion, and they do it damned well. I can put you in touch with the guy in New York who manages her account. From what you tell me, he would certainly be very interested in talking to you.'

'Sure,' thought Fleishig. 'Thanks,' he said. 'I may take you up on that.'

'I'm glad you were able to come by on such short notice, Mitchell.'

The First American Bank of Beverly Hills had closed its doors for the day. Mitchell Fleishig and Ralph Tellerson were ensconced behind Venetian blinds in a cubicle in the middle of the dark and silent ground floor of the bank headquarters on Wilshire Boulevard.

'Why did it have to be short notice, Ralph?'

Tellerson paused, visibly considering a set of equally unattractive options. His usual opening, concerning the routine review of accounts, would not wash under the circumstances. The afternoon before, his boss had come back from lunch with some story about Fleishig being desperate for money, and a little investigation revealed that he was right. Fleishig had been fudging his information to the bank, and Tellerson had not picked up on it. His boss was not pleased. If he did not recoup Fleishig's debt, Tellerson could find himself in the job market, competing with lots of hungry people twenty years younger than him.

He decided to start off in a tone that the instructor in his negotiating seminar called 'perceived candor.'

'Mitchell, you and I have been through too much together for me to lay a line on you. I have to tell you some things I don't want to say and you certainly don't want to hear. The situation is that yesterday afternoon I was called in by one of our vice-presidents to discuss your account. I put some people to work on your file, and when I reported back to the vice-president an hour ago, he told me to stabilize our position.'

'You mean you're not going to float my end of Pico Bello II?'

'I'll get to that later.'

'So get to what you have to get to first.'

'Okay, I'll tell you. What comes first is that we're calling your loan and reeling in your credit line.'

Fleishig felt as if Tellerson had hit him in the solar plexus. For this he was not prepared. Since getting the summons to appear at the bank at closing time, he had been working on the update of his ongoing story: no properties sold in three months because of recession aggravated by seasonal drop aggravated by cyclical drop, but holdings in collateral still worth 200% of outstanding debt, projected gains on Pico Bello II giving Rodeo Realty best year yet if bank will maintain current assessments. First fallback for negotiations was to a ten percent cut in assessment, leaving Rodeo barely in the black but still looking better than the competition. Second fallback was to give First American a piece of Pico Bello II. In the past, Tellerson had listened to the ongoing story respectfully, full of interest and enthusiasm. And why not? Fleishig's cash projections may not always have come out on the dollar, but he and the bank had always been able to work out mutually acceptable terms for the next turnover. Tellerson never seemed to ask the critical questions about Fleishig's projects, and Fleishig had decided that he did not have much on the ball. Bankers, he figured, did not know what really went on out there in the market. Still, they were smart enough to lend to him. Fleishig thought they were impressed by his style and his track record. They should be. How could they go wrong with someone so fine-tuned to the vibes of Beverly Hills real estate?

This reverie entered his dazed mind once more, mocking him. He felt as if he had been called to the principal's office for not doing his homework and instead of having to write excuses on the board a hundred times being put in front of a firing squad.

'Do you mean what you are saying?'

'I'm afraid so, Mitchell. I see you are taking it very hard, and it *is* serious. But it's not the end of the world, or the end of your business. We want to help you get out of the woods, while protecting ourselves.'

'But what's wrong? What's so wrong with my account today that you didn't know last time we turned over my debt?'

'It's a combination of things. For two years now you have been pushing your credit for all it's worth. You are always using all the debt you can; even forgetting about the loan, you haven't been liquid since we opened the credit line. OK, we knew this last month, but the environment is deteriorating faster than we thought. In the last quarter, our index on West Side properties lost 11 points, and the average length of time commercial real estate is on the market went up by two whole weeks. We looked at your position, and we had to conclude that the marketability of your holdings is only so-so. If we consider the fact that you haven't sold a major property in three months, we actually might be talking zero marketability in the short term.

'And we went over your assessments. I'm afraid we ran into some bad news there. Unless we are mistaken, there are serious discrepancies in the ratio of rentable footage, public areas and service space in your figures on the Redondo mall. When we made the loan we took your statements at face value. And Redondo looked so much like Baldwin Park that we accepted it when you applied the same formulas. Now that we've done a check at the registrar's we find that you seem to have overstated rentability by a good twenty to twenty-five percent. This is actionable stuff, Mitchell, but let's not talk about that. Let's just get the money back. I'm in charge of your account, and my ass is on the line too.'

Fleishig could not believe he was hearing these words from the man who would say Gee Whiz while lending him the money to buy into the properties they were talking about. But it was no use trying to get into contact with that other Tellerson this afternoon. Gee Whiz Tellerson was out to lunch, and his horrifyingly well-informed alter ego was minding the store.

'What does this mean, Ralph?'

'It means I'm going to the credit committee tomorrow, and I expect them to tell me to secure our collateral. For the time being I'm asking you not to sell any assets without consulting me first. After tomorrow we'll want all receipts from sales to come straight here. Over a period of ten weeks, we are going to

close down your credit line, ten percent a week. If you cooper-
ate, it may be possible to do this without wasting Rodeo Realty.
But right now, you're going to have to cut overhead by at least
half. That means firing staff, moving to a cheaper location, down-
grading your car and office machines, slashing expenses and not
drawing any salary. None. You will have to sell personal possessions to feed yourself. We want a meeting with you in one week
to hear what you have done, and we will be watching you in the
meanwhile.'

'Is there any point in trying to negotiate this with you?'

'You hear the answer in my voice and I hear it in yours.'

The one card Fleishig was still holding was now played for
him by Tellerson. Fleishig was no longer a player, he had become
the dummy.

'As we see it, your one marketable asset is your option in Pico
Bello II. We are going to exercise that option together. I have a
partnership contract here. You hold seventy-five percent, which
we will finance through our credit corporation at twenty-two
percent interest. We get a quarter of the equity and a full vote.
You and your wife both have to sign. Get it back to us by close
of business tomorrow.'

These people, Fleishig thought, are worse than the mob. Benny
Santangelo is a sensitive and reasonable person next to these
guys, and I'm glad he's going to kill me before these scumbags
get their money back.

'I think I might just go down with eights and jacks.'

'You sure, Beatrice?'

'I got the cards. Read 'em and weep.'

'I'm readin' 'em, but you don't see me weepin', do you?'

'Yeah, how come, Rachel?'

'Because I'm gonna lay off so much stuff on you you're gonna
think that you're me and I'm you.'

Rachel Epstein spoke through a voice box that only worked
when she pressed it. Since her left hand was dangling from her

strapped arm, tubed for dripping and draining, she had to put down her cards every time she wanted to talk. This did not seem to bother her. Nor did she notice the pained reactions of listeners to the monotone rasp that came out of the box. She spoke as much as she could. Even more than before the tracheotomy, Beatrice sometimes thought. She blamed herself for not being able to get used to the sound.

Talking was not the only thing that held up the game. To take a drag on the Marlboros she chain-smoked, Rachel had to put down her cards. To play them, she had to lay them face down on the tray and pick them up one by one. If she forgot what she was holding, she had to scoop up the cards, bring them to her left hand for fanning and sorting, and then lay them down again. She showed no signs of impatience, nor did Beatrice Fleishig.

'I gottanotha canasta. A natural. Oh, are you gonna bleed.'

The scorepad recorded all the hands that the two women had played since Rachel Epstein entered the Hospice of the Angels of Peace. Rachel was leading by twenty thousand points. She had always been a good canasta player, but in her match with her new friend Beatrice she reached new heights of mastery.

Today the game went more slowly than usual. Rachel stopped not only to talk and to fan her cards but also to sit out the pain when it got too bad. She had been receiving morphine injections daily and then twice daily since the operation, but the blanket of comfort it provided was getting patchy.

After another winning hand, Rachel sat back and looked at Beatrice.

'Have you read your mail yet, Rachel?'

'Hush, Beatrice. Lemme jus' lookatchya.'

Rachel received lots of mail, from her eighteen children. She started having them late, after her third miscarriage. Through charity organizations, she and her husband adopted foster children all over the world. They made monthly payments to the organizations, and if the recipients put the money to good use, they would continue to support them after they grew up. Many of the foster children wrote to their benefactors, in a babel of languages. The Epsteins had the letters translated, and sent back answers in the children's language. After Rachel's husband died, she cut down on the translations and reduced her end of the correspondence to birthday and New Year's cards. But most of her children kept writing and sending photographs. Some of them were parents and even grandparents. They did not know that Rachel was ill. She had written letters to each of them, to be mailed after her death, with a final amount of money to help them buy a shop or a car or a house or to pay off their debts — whatever they needed to become more independent. 'God bless the child that's got his own,' she wrote. 'Use this money in such a way that you will not need money from other people anymore. And use some of it to help other people. That will make you feel as good about your life as I feel about mine. More I cannot wish you.'

The pain came quickly and relentlessly, rising in a few seconds to a crescendo. Rachel shut her eyes and hoped that her ally morphine would drive the pain back out of the door and bolt it shut. But morphine was beaten. He was flailing around even more helplessly than Rachel, pushing against her for safety. She picked him up and comforted him. We're gonna have to leave the house, she told him. Don't worry about it. I can move back in with Eppy, and I'll tell him you have to come with me.

When she opened her eyes, Beatrice was still sitting beside the bed, her hands palm up in her lap.

'Beatrice, you are the nicest person I ever knew..I'm sorry we couldn't be friends longer.'

'We'll be friends for the rest of our lives, Rachel. There's no longer than that.'

'Gimme a hug, honey, and lemme get some rest.'

When Beatrice got home, she was surprised to find the house dark. Jean was supposed to put the lights on at twilight, and she had never forgotten before.

'Jean? Jeanie?'

Mitchell's voice came from his study.

'Jeanie's not here. I sent her home.'

Beatrice put on the lights in the living room.

'I hope it's nothing serious. Rachel Epstein is very bad, and I don't want anyone else around me to get sick. I can only take so much.'

'What the hell is that supposed to mean? You volunteer in a goddamned hospice for terminal patients, and when people start dying on you it's like you didn't know it was going to happen. What's with you, Bea? Isn't it time you grew up and got in touch with the world? Anyway, your precious Jeanie isn't sick. She went home because I fired her.'

'What?'

'You heard me. It's like talking to the wall around here. What? What? I fired Jeanie, that's what.'

'How could you do that? She was with us for years. She was like one of the family.'

'I could do it because it had to be done. And that isn't all I have to do. Give me all your credit cards and your charge cards and your checkbooks.'

'Mitchell, what's got into you? Why are you like this?'

'Look, I don't have time to talk to you all day. Obviously, as even you can see, we have run into money trouble. The bank has turned off the faucet. We do not have money to spend. None.'

'But you told me everything was going so well. Wasn't it?'

'All I need on top of everything is for you to blame me for what happened. I don't know what happened. All of a sudden the bank dropped the boom on me. Here, you have to sign these papers.'

'I'm not going to sign anything until you explain what's going on.'

'What's going on is that my whole life is coming to an end. Everything I worked for, everything I own, everything I have become, everything I was going to be. They are turning me into nothing. As if for all these years I was nothing, a nebbish, worse than your moron brother.'

'They can't do that to you just like that. You're a solid businessman. There must be something else to it. What is it?'

'There's nothing else. Just the bank.'

'You've had problems with the bank before and you always worked them out. That can't be the issue. You're not telling me the whole story.'

'The whole story is that if you don't shut up and sign these papers and give me your plastic I won't be responsible for myself. I was on the way to becoming the biggest man in West Side real estate, and I won't let them make believe I am a nothing. Whatever I have to do, I'll do.'

Altstad's bet with himself was not going well. At twenty-five, while working on his Ph.D. in art history, he had decided against pursuing the kind of career he was being trained for, in the academic world or in a museum. He made up his mind on the threshold of a luncheonette on East 86th Street the day he passed his oral examinations. To the satisfaction of three living legends of art scholarship, including a notoriously cranky and self-important medievalist who diverted himself on these occasions by trying to throw the candidate into acute collapse, Altstad had demonstrated his mastery of the field. In response to the committee's questioning, he had delivered impromptu disquisitions on Sassanian silver, the narrative strategies of Ottonian miniaturists, and the maritime and agricultural references in Greek architectural details. He compared the illusionistic devices in the ceiling paintings in German and Italian churches and palaces around 1700, larding his talk with phrases in the original languages from contemporaneous guidebooks and mystic literature; speculated on the differences in Russian Byzantinology as practiced in the Late Czarist and Early Soviet periods; and aperçued the New York School abandonment of Abstract Expressionism for Pop Art in terms of real-estate prices and neighborhood peculiarities in the West and East Village. The facts, dates and examples bubbled up on call, and he found himself able to round them off into elegant précis. His initial nervousness gave way, after half an hour of this winning act, to a feeling of invincibility. For the rest of the morning, he awaited each new question with the confidence of a champion skeet shooter who knew he never missed more than two clay pigeons out of a hundred. The medievalist grew increasingly glum, and was silenced altogether when, in an attempt to improve his mood by challenging Altstad to identify an obscure Romanesque capital from a contrasty photocopy of a murky illustration, his colleague Rubachev intervened on Altstad's behalf. 'Really, André! *I* couldn't tell you what that is, and as you know I bicycled the Romanesque pilgrimage route from Cologne to Santiago de Compostela with a Leica and a stepladder.' It was Rubachev who came out to the hallway fifteen minutes after the end of the examination to congratulate Altstad.

Altstad left the Institute alone, to savor the moment privately. He wandered aimlessly to Lexington and 86th before deciding to treat himself to a bite of food. Bursting with pride, he found a way of starting up a conversation with the middle-aged man next to him, whose graying brown beard and tweed jacket gave him the look of someone who might know what a heroic accomplishment it was to pass your orals at the Institute. The man turned out to be an anthropologist specialized in Contemporary Western Man. Although he had a Ph.D. himself, enabling him to gauge the full extent of Altstad's triumph, his congratulations seemed a bit flat.

Afterwards, Altstad was unable to make up his mind what motivated the man to say what he did. It might have been cynicism, jealousy, indifference, sadism, the inability to resist such a golden opportunity. On the other hand, it could have been an act of selfless wellwishing, a shot of salutary pain. In any case, his words burned their way into Altstad's memory together with the taste of the cheese Danish he was munching and the refill of coffee with which he was washing it down.

'Human beings have the latest and longest adolescence in the animal kingdom. It doesn't end until a good quarter of their expected life-span has gone by. At that point, most humans begin supporting themselves. They mate and have offspring like any other animal. But some, especially in our society, choose to prolong their adolescence by going to college. At an age when most of their contemporaries are responsible adults with their own households, college students live in individual cells, pairing randomly and fruitlessly, and letting their parents pay for their keep. A small number of this cohort goes on to graduate school. There they become dependent for their living and their status on a professional hierarchy which bullies and charms them into imitating the established figures. This treatment turns the adult capacities of the student against himself, leading to an increased dependency on his elders. If it takes, the student loses the ability to make normal demands of life. The need he had as a child for parental love becomes a need for approval from his professors. And he gets it, in measured doses cut with contempt. By the time you finish graduate school, your emotional metabolism is a wreck. Maybe *you* can keep it running well enough to maintain healthy relationships with other people. I couldn't.'

Starting with an anthropological generality, the well-rehearsed speech of the man at the counter had narrowed to the third person, the rhetorical second person, the second person he was talking to, and finally the first. Altstad was appalled by the man's despair and even more by his conviction that the despair was incurable, a consequence of getting out of step with his own humanity. And he thought Altstad too was taking that step. Altstad could say nothing. He gave a few short nods, not of affirmation but of acknowledgment that the message had been received, put a tip on the counter, paid and left.

On the street, he realized without having to consult his feelings that his mind was made up. Whether or not the anthropologist was right, what he said made sense to Altstad. The morning's performance was just that. He had behaved like a trained animal going through a complicated act. If there were original thoughts in anything he said, he had taken care to disguise them. All he had done was flatter the committee by reformulating their ideas in his words. What a compliment! Four years of sacrifice to shore up their authority. This was not anthropology, it was monkey-house ethology.

And four years was not the end of it. It would take him another two or three years to do a dissertation. Only then would they let him start his way up the slippery pole, taking kicks from above all the time. Assistant Professor at Sheboygan State until his first article appeared. If it made a splash, he would move up to Assistant Professor in some big midwest or southern university, and if his first book got the right reviews he could go onto tenure track at the University of California or New York or an Ivy League school. He might be forty before coming up for tenure review at a good place. Without tenure, he would be virtually unable to play a role of any importance in the field. But even if he got it, he would already have spent half his life in tutelage.

He wouldn't do it. That's all, he just wouldn't. He was going to find a way of standing on his own feet before he became any more dependent than he already was.

An immediate break was inconceivable. All he amounted to in life was the letter he would be getting from the Institute certifying the completion of his course work and exams for the Ph.D. A worthless piece of paper, but he did not have the strength to tear it up. Did anyone?

He would do his dissertation in no more than two years, weaning himself in a simultaneous counter-movement from the Alma Mater. By the time he finished, he wanted to be ready for unmediated contact with the world at large. He would be his own man.

As the subject of his doctoral thesis, Altstad chose the most concrete subject he could get away with, against the aggressive current of theory that was washing away or staining everything in its path. With a defiance of academic fashion that Rubachev secretly admired, Altstad wrote five hundred solid pages on topography in Dutch cityscape painting. He identified the buildings, streets and canals in two hundred prints and one hundred paintings of Amsterdam, Haarlem and Delft, putting them into a matrix of dates and localities covering the seventeenth and eighteenth centuries. He tabulated every significant element in each depiction, classifying them in a system he constructed out of the chapter divisions of period guidebooks. For each locality and each type of building, he quoted all the references from the standard town descriptions and as many passages as he could find in the writings of Dutch poets and playwrights and the journals of foreign visitors. Previous researchers, even though they could generally identify the sites, tended to miss out on minor but often telltale discrepancies in the representations. Altstad corrected the observations of his predecessors politely, but only when he could back up his revisions with such solid proof that no further argument was possible.

With an obstinacy bordering on defiance, Altstad refused to draw conclusions from his findings. He pointed out patterns and correlations where they sprang to the eye, but would not assign a meaning to them. He claimed not to know whether the blossoming of architectural painting in Delft in the 1650s was related to city politics, national politics, religion or an internal art-world mechanism. Even when seventeenth-century authors spoke of cause and effect, Altstad would quote them without commentary.

He refused to follow the fellow students who entered the never-neverland of the new art history or critical theory, where nothing was as it seemed. For them, a city was not a city, it was a metaphor of society, a public theater for private lives, a reification of a power structure, a palimpsest of history, a cultural construct, a petrified parable or a psycho-social fantasy. Nor was a townscape primarily a view in a city. Rather, it was a visual valorization, ratification, privileging, canonization or reassertion of one kind of discourse, and a revocation, depreciation, critiquing or querying of another. Altstad did not comment on their ideas in his dissertation, not even in the notes. In discussion, they would listen incredulously to his description of his project. 'But what's your *project*?' they would ask, indicating that they could stoop to countenance his apparent naiveté if he would provide it with a political or philosophical subtext. He made believe he didn't understand. 'I just told you,' he would say. 'Identifying the places.' They soon stopped talking to him.

He was able to continue talking to colleagues of the historicist inclination, but it was one-way communication. They looked at cityscapes mainly for the artist's choice of motifs, which they related to the interests of the burghers and institutions that bought the paintings. The historicists were keen to use Altstad's information, which he provided freely. But he would not talk to them about their ideas. When they asked him what he thought about the links between the function of the buildings in the paintings and the biographies of the artist and his buyers, he would reply noncommittally. 'I haven't thought much about that,' he would say, or 'That's a fascinating possibility.'

Nor did Altstad's work pay allegiance to the cherished values of his teachers. There were no chapters or even paragraphs on space, light or tonality. The older generation, when they noticed a deliberate departure from topographical accuracy in a cityscape, would explain it in aesthetic terms. The artist was improving on reality for the sake of a better composition, they would say, assuming the role of the artist's drawing teacher for the occasion. Altstad did not use this argument. He did not attempt to explain the artist's motives in any way at all.

Even more frustrating was that Altstad demurred to attach an artist's name to an unsigned, undocumented work. Most of the prints were incised with the name of the artist who drew the scene and the printmaker who engraved or etched it. Altstad accepted these at face value. But only about one in ten of the paintings bore a convincing inscription or was otherwise documented as being the work of a specific individual. The other ninety percent, including paintings from the oldest collections and the best museums, works whose attribution to some famous artist had never been questioned before, were catalogued by Altstad as 'Attributed to' Vrel or Berckheyde or Ouwater, as the case may be. In the introduction, he explained that he did not intend to cast doubt on the traditional attributions, but merely to make clear which were based on documentary authentication and which were inferred from stylistic evidence.

'You know as well as I do what it means when you say in a catalogue raisonné that a work is "attributed,"' Rubachev remarked in annoyance.

'Yes, I do. It means that the author does not think the work is by the master to whom he says he is attributing it. In other words, that it's not attributed to the master. All I'm doing is restoring to the word its literal meaning.'

Only once did Altstad drop his guard in a talk with Rubachev, and give a reason for his resistance.

'I want to be able to back up everything I say with my own authority.'

'Your own authority? That's not what scholarship is about, my young friend. Whatever authority you possess is on license to you from the field. If you want to command credence, you have to use the concepts and terminology that the rest of us use. You have to take the same chances we all do. You have to stick out your neck on attributions and interpretations, even if you have no more to go on than your instinct. That's what we've been trying to do with you here — sharpen your instincts, so when you give your measured opinion on a moot point in your special area, the rest of us can follow you on it. Aside from questions of right and wrong, taking those kinds of chances is a demonstration of intellectual collegiality that the field will appreciate and reward.'

Altstad had tipped his hand, and had to back down before Rubachev caught on to the full measure of his recalcitrance. It was exactly what Rubachev called 'intellectual collegiality' that Altstad wanted to eliminate from his work, that whole sticky mess of unargued assumptions, in-crowd buzzwords and subjective judgments that art historians conspired silently to respect in each other's writings. Altstad had learned it well enough. He had a talented journeyman's sense of what the consensus would credit, what it would question, and what it would decry. But the anthropologist's message had made him decide not to play the game. To do so would perpetuate his dependence on his elders indefinitely, even if he left art history. He would have collaborated with their regime, demonstrated that he was willing to subject the workings of his mind to their arbitrary demands. The only way he could get a Ph.D. with his head high would be to write a dissertation based on criteria that any sensible human being could understand, with arguments that would stand on their own in any court. This meant rejecting all the intellectual shortcuts that his training put at his disposal. In replying to Rubachev, he tried to make it sound more innocent.

'What I wanted to do was offer the users of my work very solid assurance that they could go on what I tell them.'

'For documented facts from the archives we don't need your personal assurance. Nobody expects one hundred percent certainty in art history. We're dealing with gradual shades of artistic worth and meaning, and all we ask from each other is to attune to them as best we can.'

'Yes, I see that. Perhaps I'm being too timid. [Too insolent, he thought but did not say.] I'll try to put more of my own judgment in my work.'

He didn't. The dissertation defense was a drama.

'Mr. Altstad,' the medievalist pontificated, 'this is not a vocational school for archivists or a hobby center for collecting postcards of old buildings. We study art here, and we take the demands of art seriously. If you do not wish to join us in this high endeavor, you simply have no business being here.'

It took all of Rubachev's authority and credit with his colleagues to rescue Altstad's degree from the jaws of death. This time he was in the corridor not for fifteen minutes but for three hours before his exhausted, disgusted supervisor emerged from conclave.

'This would have been easier if I believed full-heartedly in the cause. But I don't. I think you're being a bloody-minded ass. The reason I did it is that I once had faith in you. You have a good mind, and it would be a pity to see you end up in the gutter.'

By that time, although Rubachev did not know it, Altstad already had one foot in the gutter, as defined by the mandarins of the Institute. He was working for an art dealer.

He met Willem Molenaar while writing his dissertation. After studying the materials in the topographical atlases of the municipal archives of Amsterdam, Haarlem and Delft and in the Center for Art History in The Hague, he heard that an Amsterdam art dealer had a photo archive with a strong section on cityscape paintings. Molenaar received him courteously and gave him the free run of his collection.

Altstad did not expect much. How could the clippings of an art dealer who was not even an art historian compare with the holdings of municipal archives or the august Center for Art History? He was astonished and chastened by what he found. It was the institutions who collected by ad hoc criteria, and Molenaar who put together a systematic documentation. The archives and the Center filed what they inherited or what was given to them. Molenaar went after his material, inserting it into a twofold system under artist and subject. For the artist files, Molenaar had cut up copies of expensive scholarly catalogues — in most cases two copies, since the illustrations were printed back to back, while a third copy, filled with marginal notes, would be on his shelf of monographs. This provided him with a system in which every known or reported work by the master was represented, not just those for which photographs or illustrations from museum and auction-house catalogues were available.

The subject files, for Molenaar's section on cityscapes, were photographs of the illustrations, arranged street by street and building by building. That was also the system in the municipal archives. The difference was that they were after visual documentation of buildings, while Molenaar was interested in artistic motifs. The archives filed photographs and newspaper clippings alongside paintings, prints and drawings. Undocumented addresses were lacunae waiting to be filled in. In Molenaar's collection, which contained only works of art, the white spots on the map were not inconveniences, they were hard information, the negative traces of the activities of artists who crowded each other out to make yet another view of the tourist attractions and the houses of important patrons and turned their backs on the rest of the city, however picturesque it may have been.

That was not the only one of Altstad's preformed ideas that

Molenaar overturned. Altstad thought that a dealer in artists' reputations would feel threatened by an art historian who was as fastidious as he was about distinguishing between authenticated and attributed works. But Molenaar was almost shockingly laconic when he saw the manuscript of Altstad's catalogue.

'That's quite a useful distinction,' he said.

Altstad's sense of relief was cosmic. The cloud of academic pretension from which he was desperate to emerge was pierced by a ray of simple illumination. He followed it, and found that Molenaar had as much to offer as Rubachev, and asked for less in return. What's more, when he asked for something he paid for it. After years of student subsistence, living on fellowships that made the poverty line look like the Emerald City, Altstad was earning the kind of money you could actually spend on things you wanted. Molenaar paid him a decent hourly rate for research on paintings coming up for auction, entries for his catalogues and captions for photographs in his archive.

Watching Molenaar operate, the prejudices that were bred into Altstad against trading in objects he was taught to revere were gradually dispelled. Museum curators from all over Europe and America would drop in for a look at some new work on offer, and over coffee they would chat amicably and respectfully with the dealer. Although Molenaar cultivated a modest style, it was obvious to Altstad that he knew more about the paintings than the curators did. He passed on to them rules of thumb ('In a van der Heyden townscape you can count the bricks, in Berckheyde you can barely see the courses') that would have been sneered out of class in the Institute, but which worked perfectly well in practice, and for which the curators were grateful.

Altstad settled into Molenaar's library, working part time on his dissertation while doing odd jobs for the dealer. One day, at a preview of an auction at the Amsterdam Old York gallery, a spark jumped from one of his worlds to the other. He and Molenaar were looking at an Amsterdam harbor scene catalogued as 'School of Jacob van Ruisdael.' This was a weak designation that would depress the bidding.

'A case could be made for Reinier Nooms,' Altstad mumbled.

Molenaar, who was already moving to the next painting, stopped dead in his tracks.

'Tell me more.'

'Nooms drew this stretch of the Damrak for an unexecuted etching. The drawing is more horizontal and includes another few buildings on the left, but the details correspond pretty closely, as I recall.'

A look at Altstad's photograph of the drawing revealed that they did, and a bit more searching turned up a reference to a painting of the subject by Nooms, with the identical dimensions, in a good early eighteenth-century collection. Altstad and Molenaar compared an auction-house photograph with the paintings by Nooms in the Maritime Museum and convinced themselves that they were by the same hand. Molenaar bought the painting at the sale for eleven thousand guilders.

'Half of the difference between what I paid and what I get when I sell the painting is yours, Lodewijk. You earned it.'

Under the new attribution, backed up by Altstad's arguments, the painting soon found a buyer for eighty thousand guilders. Altstad took five thousand guilders in cash and put the rest into shares of paintings in Molenaar's gallery. Molenaar filled him in on the prognoses for profit and saleability of each of the paintings Altstad picked out, and opened his eyes to the investment value of some others, paintings Altstad had not looked at closely because they were not interesting to art history.

Reinvesting most of his profits as Molenaar sold the paintings in which he had a share, Altstad soon had a portfolio worth more than a hundred thousand guilders. He could not help realizing that in half a year of part-time work he had made nearly as much money trading in art as Rubachev, twice his age, earned in a year of teaching.

On a visit with Molenaar to the house of a collector with a flower still-life to sell, Altstad was attracted to a male portrait signed by the Utrecht painter Jan van Bijlert. On the way back to the Rokin, Altstad asked him why he showed no interest in the portrait, which he thought was a finer painting than the still-life.

'In terms of quality and condition, you're right. The trouble is, there is not much of a market either for portraits or for the Utrecht school. If I were younger I might start developing those areas, but in my position it would be foolish. People come to me for real collector's paintings — still lifes, landscapes, conversation pieces, you know what I sell. For these I am able to charge good prices. It would only confuse my buyers if I offered better quality paintings for less money. But if you ever want to start on your own, that could be an interesting possibility. You would have to educate your collectors, but you'd be good at that.'

Altstad was intrigued. Molenaar lent him the money to buy the van Bijlert, against Altstad's share in some of his own stock. He was in business for himself.

Altstad's conversion was exhilarating, but it also brought its pangs of conscience. Was he not prostituting his talents for money, and degrading art by buying and selling it? He quelled his reservations with powerful — perhaps too powerful — arguments. As an art historian, he had pretended that the art on the screen, in the books and on the museum walls somehow belonged to him and to all of humanity. Now he told himself that while the images may in some sense be the property of mankind, the objects certainly weren't. They were chattel, and as a dealer he had a much more realistic relationship to them than as a scholar. This did not preclude respect. In fact, it was more respectful, since it also entailed responsibility for the physical survival of the works he handled. Even the study of art, for a dealer, meshed with reality in a more satisfying way than for an academic. Instead of mouthing noncommittal pieties and speculations, a dealer risked good money on his convictions. Dealers were less afraid to look truth in the face. Wasn't the superiority of Molenaar's archive proof that this attitude actually led to a purer, less tendentious form of knowledge than in the university? How old was the university, anyway? Academic art history was barely one hundred and fifty years old. And who was taking care of art scholarship before that? Dealers, mainly. Altstad was proud to join their ranks.

Entering the art trade was the second part of Altstad's answer to the anthropologist in the luncheonette. The first was the method of his dissertation, which would stand on its merits with or without the approval of the top apes at the Institute. That was the hard part. The second was amazingly, unexpectedly quick and easy. He was paying his own way in life, and could tell his mentors what to do with their fellowships, assistant professorships and tenure tracks. He had broken out of the chrysalis.

Still, Altstad's bet with himself was not going well. Rumbling under the East River on the Flushing Local, he was overcome by the sickening fear that he was going to lose it. The term for the bet was about to lapse, and things were looking bad. When he decided not to look for work in the field for which he had been trained, he knew he was taking a big chance. As a safeguard against kidding himself into believing this was not so, he gave himself three years to make good in life.

He took the challenge very literally. His anthropological reasons for not going into the academic world were concrete: to stay out of the hands of a bunch of intellectual bullies and to be able to love. If the art trade did not bring him financial independence and emotional stability, then it would be more destructive than life as an academic. He took his thirtieth birthday as the cut-off date. By then he had to have reached two milestones: he had to be clearing at least as much as a university job would have earned him, and he had to have (or at least had to have had) a good, lasting relationship with a woman. If not, he would admit defeat and get back into line.

It seemed like a sure thing at the time. It seemed like a sure thing until a week before the subway ride, three weeks before he would turn thirty, if he lived that long. Then it crumbled, just like that. In Amsterdam he met with his accountant to go over last year's figures. It had seemed to Altstad like a terrific year. He sold eight paintings and had earned more than a hundred percent profit on them. His costs were low, and he had been able to draw a decent salary from his one-man firm and take out a mortgage on a small apartment in Amsterdam without having to cash in any of his shares in Molenaar's stock. In fact, he had increased those holdings, plowing his take from Molenaar's sales back into some more expensive paintings. Most important, he had been able to upgrade his own stock with some terrific, underpriced pastoral landscapes he bought from a German collector who was moving from paintings to books.

He was honestly surprised by the accountant's concerned tone.

'How are your prospects for this year, Mr. Altstad?'

'Well, the market is pretty rocky, so I may not do as well as last year. But I don't have to, do I? I earned very well last year, and that should tide me over for a while.'

'What do you mean? Is there something you've kept off the books?'

Altstad was jolted. He was perfectly content with what was *on* the books, and had come in expecting a bit of quiet admiration from the accountant.

'Your capital is all tied up in stock, in a market that you say yourself is slowing down. If the paintings you and Mr. Molenaar are holding have not sold yet, why do you think they are going to sell now?'

It was an infuriatingly stupid question for which Altstad unfortunately did not have an answer.

'But even if I value the stock at what you paid for it, once I take off the mortgage and your back taxes you still have a negative capital. If I were reviewing your books for a credit rating, I would have to conclude that you are virtually bankrupt.'

Seeing Altstad's total confusion, the accountant, in an effort to be helpful, asked him the question that wiped out three years of spectacular progress.

'You once told me you had a university degree in art history. Couldn't you take a teaching job? It would give you more security.'

In the week that had gone by since this devastating revelation, Altstad's worth had not increased. He had sunk all his cash and more into a painting of an ugly monster. He had also lied to the *Kensington*, bluffed the ring, used the unwitting Molenaar's name to cover himself while shutting his mentor out of the first decent deal that had come his way, and written a check to Old York that he wasn't sure he could cover. A trail of booby traps ready to blow him up. If his accountant hadn't told him he was in trouble, he would have figured it out by now all by himself. Or was he behaving recklessly because of the accountant?

But what his accountant told him last week did not shake him as much as what Katy had said yesterday. Katy, for a whole year the living proof that he *could* love, let him know that he was carrying on an affair with a half-imaginary woman. A wonderful woman was in love with him, and what does he do? Look through her to her shadow, whose contours he filled out from his fantasy.

Apparently the anthropologist's warning had come too late. For all the chance he had to escape the legacy of prolonged adolescence, he might as well save himself the trouble. He was better off settling up with Molenaar and going on his knees to Rubachev to beg for a recommendation for an assistant professorship in the deep boonies. He would get married to another neurotic art historian and fight with her for the rest of his life. He thought of calling Rubachev when he got off the train to make an appointment.

That he did not knuckle under then and there was not due to a resurgence of morale at the Hunterspoint Avenue station in Long Island City. Altstad simply recalled with deepened self-contempt that he wasn't thirty yet and did not have the right to give up and let go.

The cashier at the 24-hour diner was expecting him. Katy and Emma Rae were regulars there. They each kept a pair of roller blades in the back room to skate to their loft. The streets were empty and broad enough to evade an attacker if you were moving quickly. Their studio was in an abandoned factory building, with no telephone and no doorbell. Katy had left a key for Altstad at the diner.

'You pronounce your name different than Katy. She said something like Lo-de-vike. You say the v softer and the i in ike goes from eh to ay. We have lots of Dutch names around this neighborhood. We probably pronounce all of them wrong. Right around the corner is Van Alst Street.' She pronounced both A's the same, a broad A as in Van Heflin. 'How do the Dutch say Van Alst?'

Altstad obliged, and the woman behind the cash register repeated it very well, with the weak vowel of the unaccented 'van' and the long, nasal double A of Aalst, the highpoint of the name, which the Americans had removed from the spelling and the sound both.

'From now on I'm going to impress everybody with my authentic Dutch accent. They won't know what I'm talking about.'

Altstad walked along 49th Avenue to the bridge over the dead-end canal called Dutch Kills. A few blocks beyond it was Van Dam Street. Altstad guessed that the Kills once separated large farms belonging to two Dutch landowners named van Aalst and van Dam. He tried to picture the land as it had then looked, with no effect except to deepen his depression. The building with Katy's studio overlooked the water. He let himself in, found the flashlight where Katy said it would be, and bolted the door behind him. Before climbing to the loft he sat down on the stairs to gather his thoughts.

Altstad's relationship with Katy Eskenazi was the longest he had ever had. Although he was in New York for only about one week each month, neither of them thought of it as a part-time affair. To Altstad, Katy was a miracle. She was helping him to ease himself into maturity and marriage. At least, that's what he thought she was doing until yesterday.

He had met her and her friend Emma Rae a year before in front of a Vermeer at the Metropolitan Museum of Art. It was not one of the Metropolitan's standard Vermeers, the woman with the jug, the sleeping maid or the girl's head. The painting in front of which Altstad had been joined by two intense young women was one that most people passed by in silence, *An Allegory of the Catholic Religion*. In a Dutch interior revealed by a drawn-back Flemish tapestry, a seated woman, beautifully dressed in blue, white and gold, wearing a string of pearls, holds a hand to her breast and gazes upward in rapture. Her sandaled right foot rests high on a big globe. Behind her is a large painted *Crucifixion with Mary, John and an Angel*; the table on which she leans is almost an altar for the mass, with a chalice, a holy book and a bronze Christ on a tall, ebony Cross, standing out dramatically against a red and gold leather screen. The woman and the table are on a low, carpeted platform, occupying the back right quadrant of the floor. On the floor itself, a broken checkerboard of black and veined white marble tiles, are an apple with one bite missing and a snake crushed to bloody death beneath a large stone block beside a chair with a high cushion. A glass sphere dangles from the beamed ceiling on a blue velvet ribbon over the woman's head.

The *Allegory* is given short shrift by art historians, who avoid discussing it if they can. It was an undisputed Vermeer, but not a real one. A real Vermeer is true to life, this one is stylized and contains impossible details; Vermeer is a *visual* painter, and the *Allegory* is based on emblems from a book. Dutch art is supposed to be Calvinistic or secular, and here is an unabashedly Catholic painting by the Dutchest of Dutch masters — himself a Catholic. Art historians were ill at ease with these inconvenient facts. They faulted Vermeer for having delivered an uncharacteristic product. They criticized the execution of the painting, claiming to be disappointed by the lighting or the composition. In an effort to spare their hero, they decided that Vermeer did not invent the composition himself. He must have made it, they wrote, for a Catholic patron who induced him to betray his own nature. No art historian had ever written about the extremely high value placed upon the painting by Vermeer's contemporaries. In the same decade as the *View of Delft* was sold at auction for 200 guilders, the *Allegory* fetched 400. This was almost ten times more than the worth accorded to the *Allegory of Painting* in Vienna, which art historians worshipped. Altstad relished their discomfort with the *Allegory of the Catholic Religion*. He never skipped it on his visits to the Met, savoring it as proof that present-day taste was a rotten guide to what past ages considered quality in art. It was a living vindication of his own way of doing art history, without aesthetic conjecture.

As he stood before it that day, renewing the warrant for his resistance to the teachings of Rubachev, he was distracted by two female voices beside him. He was used to the comments on this painting by the few visitors who paused to look at it. Nothing in their art appreciation courses prepared them for a Vermeer that was not a celebration of the everyday. The usual visitors covered their confusion with conventional praise for the painter's skill in creating space and depicting different kinds of fabrics and surfaces, and moved on as quickly as appearances permitted. But the women beside him that day did not move on, nor did they make embarrassed noises. Altstad listened in astonishment as they praised the painting exactly for the qualities that art historians found so indigestible.

'Look at that woman! She's fantastic. God, is she beautiful. Look how strong she is, but so happy. She has her foot on a globe. She's like on top of the world. That's how happy she is. Look at that powerful little smile. Her eyes are on fire, and her body is so luscious she can't keep her hands off herself. Oooh, she has it *all*.'

'And she's so self-contained. She's in the middle of the room, but she's also in a space all her own. She has her own color and her own world of light. She's glowing, but at the same time she's so cool.'

'Do you see what's going on? I can't believe it! There's a dead snake on the floor. Is that a phallic symbol or what? And it's dead, she crushed the beast and that's why she's so happy.'

'Yeah, that's a stream of sick red blood coming out of the picture towards us. You feel like wiping it away. What do you suppose the apple is doing there? Someone took a bite out of it and threw it on the floor.'

'Hey, I'm getting it. A snake, an apple, a woman. This is awesome. She's got to be Mother Eve. The snake was trying to make her give the apple to Adam. Adam must have bitten the apple. Only . . .' a tone of doubt entered the self-assured voice, 'there's no Adam here, so that doesn't figure.'

'But there's Jesus Christ.'

'Holy shit, you're right. This is deep. Jesus Christ is *dead*. He's double dead. *He* must have eaten the apple. He got killed for eating it, the snake got killed for offering it, and only she is alive and pure. Imagine that. In all the other pictures of Adam and Eve, she always gets the blame. This artist showed it like it is. Men are always laying a guilt trip on *us* for their own fucking weaknesses. Here *they* suffer the consequences, and she triumphs. This is the picture I've been looking for all my life. Mother Eve in ecstasy. Who painted it? It must be a woman.'

'The label says Johannes Vermeer, Dutch school, 1632-1675. It's a man. I've heard of him.'

'Maybe they're wrong. I'll bet they read the signature wrong, and it was really painted by a woman artist called Johanna Vermeer. Jo-Anne.'

Altstad could contain himself no longer.

'Actually, it isn't signed at all. But it has so much in common with other paintings by Johannes Vermeer that no one has ever doubted that he painted it. It's also mentioned in documents from the artist's period.'

'How can they be sure that his wife didn't paint it? They did that a lot, and the women never got the credit.'

'We have enough information about Vermeer's wife to be sure she couldn't have been a painter.'

'How come you know so much about it?'

The speaker was the taller of the two women. She was built like the woman in the painting, sturdy and broad-shouldered. Her hair too was brown, tied up in a bun and a braid. She wore a U.S. Army fatigue suit over a T-shirt printed with one of Georgia O'Keeffe's erotic buds. When she turned to him, Altstad was disconcerted by the movement of her large, beautiful-looking breasts, nipples erect, under the tight T-shirt.

'Well, I'm an art historian, my special field is Dutch art from the century of Vermeer, and I'm Dutch myself.'

Despite these impressive qualifications, Altstad heard a defensive note in his voice.

'All right, so it was painted by a man. But how did he know so much about Mother Eve?'

'I'm sorry to say that your interpretation of the painting is wrong. We happen to know that it represents . . .'

'Wait a second. Hold on, Joe. You can't stand there and tell me my interpretation of the painting is wrong.'

She imitated Altstad, making him sound like a pedantic idiot. She was talking quite loudly by now, and Altstad looked around nervously in the hope that no one he knew was in the gallery.

'I don't give a shit what kind of Dutch hotshot art historian you are, you can't tell me that woman isn't Mother Eve. I've got eyes just the same as you, and that's what I see.'

A guard came over and asked the woman to lower her voice. Before she could reply, her friend took her hand and pulled her around. Her voice was soft but unyielding. She spoke with a decided irony that was nonetheless not sarcastic.

'Emma Rae, why don't we go to the cafeteria with this gentleman. I'm sure he can tell us interesting things about the painting, even if we don't agree with him.'

The second woman was short, with long black curls framing a classic Mediterranean face, the large features delineated as clearly as if they were carved. She was not as aggressively sexy as her friend, but the lines of her green plissé blouse showed an exciting entasis that set Altstad on fire. 'My Bronchorst,' he thought, and fell in love.

To both of them, it seemed like a nice beginning for the love of an art historian for an artist. Now, in the stairwell at Dutch Kills, he saw it as a foretaste of the ambiguity that was bothering Katy so much. He dusted himself off and dragged himself up six flights of stairs to the top floor of the building. As he opened the door to the vestibule a deafening bell went off, which stopped only when the door was shut behind him. Emma Rae shouted to him from the next room.

'The art historian comes to where the history of art begins. This is where it all starts, this is the big bang. Dutchman, hold on to your crotch.'

The light in Emma Rae's studio was blinding. Her man John, who worked on the floor below, had tapped into a power line under the pavement, and fixed the studios up with lighting. Emma Rae worked with two banks of night lights from the football field of a closed-down high school. Shielding his eyes, Altstad saw at his feet a field of bright red. At first he thought it was a reaction to the light, but then he saw that it was painted, and that it was not a field but a wavy band. He followed it towards the wall. The red ribbon wound its way up, growing broader and brighter. When Altstad's gaze reached eye level, he found himself looking straight at the crushed head of a snake. The ribbon was its blood. Altstad leaped away from the wall, and as he did the floor of Vermeer's *Allegory* opened around him, covering the floor, ceiling and one long wall of the studio. He spun as he landed, falling on his butt below the short wall. Looking up, he saw a larger-than-life woman seated in the pose of Vermeer's Catholic Religion, her right foot on a globe. But the figure was completely naked, and his eye was drawn irresistibly to its center: the vagina, the lips open between the splayed legs. The model, he had no doubt, was the artist. There was an insistent fleshliness about the image that put him off, although Emma Rae always gave him a charge.

'Wow, that's the kind of reaction I want. Mother Eve knocks them off their feet.'

Katy knelt beside him, kissing him tenderly.

'Is anything wrong, little lover? Are you okay?'

'I'm all right. Just a little dizzy.'

She stood him up and looked at him closely.

'You're a bit out of it, Lodewijk. I've never seen you like this before.' She sounded concerned, but also pleased. She took his arm and walked him around the room.

'What do you think about the way Emma Rae used the painting by Vermeer?'

'I think it's very interesting.'

'Interesting?' Emma Rae thundered.

'A goddess knocks him on his ass and he calls it interesting.
What would you say if she raped you? Thought-provoking,
maybe? It isn't your thoughts we want to provoke, mister.'

'We'll see you later, Emma Rae,' Katy sang breezily, and led
Altstad to her studio in the adjoining room. They entered it
by drawing back a heavy curtain which Emma Rae had built
into her composition. The light on the other side was so dim
that at first Altstad could see nothing. Katy stood beside him
quietly as his eyes adjusted to the dark. A bright vertical line
began emerging towards his right. It was the edge of a large
canvas hanging from the ceiling. But it wasn't a line that was
painted. Second by second, his sight took in more and more
of the truth. The line was only the brightest edge of an ex-
panse of color darkening steadily leftwards from brightest
orange to deeper and deeper red. He could not see whether
there was a left edge or whether the painting disappeared off
the spectrum into pitch blackness on the left. If it did, he wondered where the canvas stopped. Or whether it stopped. For
all he could see, the descent into darkness might continue indefinitely. It was a disquieting sensation, but he said nothing
about it. He had reacted emotionally enough already to Emma
Rae's painting. Of course he knew that Katy's canvas had to
have an end.

It took nearly five minutes before he saw it. It was just as sharp
as the right edge — a line of deep purple that stood out from the
black shadows behind.

He was about to comment on the wonderful intensity of the
experience when his relief was disturbed once more. Now that
he could see the whole canvas for what it was, he realized that
there was a piece missing. Near the center, a downward-point-
ing equilateral triangle was cut out. He had not noticed it earlier
because what he saw through the neat hole was exactly the part

of the spectrum that belonged there. He wondered how Katy had managed this. Was there a small canvas behind the large one, or a second, complete version? He walked to the right edge of the painting to peep behind it. Katy watched him in suspense.

A few feet behind the painting of the red spectrum was another, the same size, hung in the same way. But to Altstad's astonishment, it was a mirror image of the first painting, going from deep purple on the right to orange on the left. Why didn't he notice the reversal in the cut-out triangle? He walked back to the front painting and stared at the hole. It still looked the way he saw it at first. Even knowing that the spectrum was going in the opposite direction, he could not see it that way. He went back and forth a few times, unable to explain to himself what he was seeing.

Katy was delighted.

'It works. You are the first person to see it without knowing what it was, and it hit you exactly the way I hoped it would. Even though the color shift is perfectly constant, you don't see it in small areas, especially in the middle. I discovered it by accident, and decided to take a chance. Here, this is for you.'

Katy handed him an orange canvas triangle, laid down on a square of black linoleum flecked with a red that matched the orange beautifully, like the colors in a blood orange.

'The linoleum was left over from Emma Rae's project. She painted it on exactly 999 tiles. You only saw part of it. It's humongous. She can cover a gym with it or put it into a closet. It's very scary in a closet. She'll make something different out of it every time she installs it, but it will always be called 'Mother Eve.' This is a tile she began to paint before she realized that she was finished. I call it 'The Thousandth Tile.' Only you know what it is.'

The truth of this bothered Altstad. Indeed, only he and Katy and maybe Emma Rae knew what it was, or which of its sides was up. A triangle on a square was the kind of abstract object that should stand on its own, without explanation. He had taken that tack in sometimes acrimonious arguments with fellow art-history students, and he never backed down. But the reason why 'The Thousandth Tile' moved him so deeply would never be known to anyone else, or if they did know it, they would not feel it. Discarded material from two vast works by two women, one loved and one feared, put together by the loved one as a present for him. If no one else's eye could ever see this, was it art? He knew it was.

What bothered him more was that his faith in his own eye was shaken. He had seen optical illusions before, but never had he been hit so hard by his inability to *see* something right in front of his nose. And it was not just anything. It was exactly the kind of artistic subtlety he thought he could see so well. His bet with himself was based on his superior ability to see what a painter was doing with color, not only in the arrangement of entire compositions but also in nearly microscopic details. Until now, he *knew* that he could see those sure, delicate touches of mastery that distinguished an original from a copy. Now he knew that he couldn't. Katy had demonstrated to him that his self-reliance was a delusion. But if he couldn't trust his own eyes, what could he trust?

'I'd love to go back to the city with you, but I have to keep working. I think I have the lighting right now, and I have to measure it very exactly. It was great that you came. Your reaction was just what I needed. Now I can finalize the specs. We have to pass Emma Rae's studio to get to the door. Do you think you can handle one more close encounter?'

'I guess I have to.'

Emma Rae was ready for him. In the time it took him to cross her studio and the vestibule, she got off her parting shot.

'You know what your problem is, Dutchman? For you art has to be one thing or another. But it isn't. Art is pure idea *and* pure form *and* pure thing. *Mother Eve* is a living goddess and — forgive me, Mother — a lump of shit. If you're too uptight to accept that, it's too fucking bad for you.'

The bell went off. As Katy kissed Altstad goodbye in the open doorway, Emma Rae shouted above the racket: 'Relax or die, Dutchman.'

The next morning, Altstad was not himself. Or rather, he was himself but also someone else. Someone else looking through his eyes, and seeing things differently. It started spectacularly, when he woke up and looked past his feet at the Bronchorst. He saw the painting, even saw that it was the New York version, but he also saw the girl, half-naked, exciting him beyond control. His body stiffened, blood rushed to his head, his left hand moved to a cock that in an instant was harder and hotter than he had ever known it, and the next moment he spurted semen into his face. His spine and neck arched as his pelvis bridged high, his cock still throbbing and running over. A shriek came out of him as he fell to one side and began to squirm and gasp. He saw nothing but blinding golden arcs that issued greater and greater emanations in time with his convulsions. His ears filled with a fluid rush and, dimly, his own cries. He gagged and collapsed onto the bed, still clutching himself. Masturbation was never like this. It was like being fucked by an angel of the Lord. Amazing grace. Could he ever make Katy feel that way?

He was still wondering what had happened to him when he went on his morning walk. He took the long loop to the East Park Drive and back. It was a walk like no other he had ever taken. His movements were fluid and economical, and he seemed to experience them directly, sensing the momentum and inertia of his own mass, the operations of muscles and tendons that otherwise just did their work, the weight of limbs and organs rising and falling with his steps. He was aware of his breathing and even his heartbeat, which responded to his pace in a way that seemed satisfying and inexplicably logical. The people he passed were more interesting than he had ever realized. Everyone had a unique combination of clothes, facial expression, build and gait, in countless degrees of coordination and disjointment. As the woman with the headset approached him, he saw that she was from California. The black jogging suit she was wearing he knew only from the Palisades in Santa Monica and the beach at Santa Cruz, and her headband had the colors of the Los Angeles Rams. (How did he know that?) That must be why she was not wearing a cap and why she took longer strides and looked more at ease than the New Yorker of her length and build he had passed near the armory. From closer by, he recognized her as an aerobics instructor he had seen on a Los Angeles television program the year before, on the cable net in his hotel. No wonder she could outwalk him, she was a professional. No shame in that. He flashed her a fan's shy smile.

The weather had not changed since the day before, and Altstad wondered why he had not then realized how complex it was. At every corner, turn and dip there was a change of air. The wind came from different directions with varying force, the temperature went up or down dramatically, and the atmosphere modulated. Midway through the park he came upon an eddy of old air twirling under a bridge and around a group of trees. It had gotten dustier and warmer since last month, and smelled more strongly of newsprint and chives. Further toward the west side he entered a cold continental stream straight from the mountains, with traces of agricultural and industrial scents that must have come from Pennsylvania and New Jersey. The vegetation was different here. The grass was grayer and had fewer speckles than grass out of the wind. There were toadstools he saw nowhere else in the city, growing in a pattern that defined the goblet-shaped bed of the air current across a small meadow and up the facing slope to the east.

Altstad's wonderment at New York nature was interrupted by the sight, in the entrance to the tunnel under the East Park Drive, of a strikingly colorful woman. Her overcoat was pinned full with small scraps and swatches of fabric. The materials were from everywhere — orlon from Kowloon, llama wool, Indian cashmere, wild silk from Shantung, North Carolina muslin —

and in every quality. What was the same was the color: a wild profusion of reds pushing against the uppermost end of the range of visible light. Probably beyond it as well. Altstad surmised with delight that some of the shreds might give off infrared rays, in a touch worthy of the medieval sculptors who mounted holy carvings in parts of a church no mortal eye could see. The patches formed a battlefield of clashing reds, but the figure as a whole looked like a flame. Entranced, Altstad slowed to a standstill.

Surrounded by a circle of bulging red plastic shopping bags, the woman was leaning against the outside tunnel wall, putting on her makeup. She had caked her face and forehead with deep rouge, and was now applying scarlet lipstick. Her chin, cheeks and upper lip were already covered unevenly, and she was now ready to do her lips. Her eyes were closed and she had pursed her mouth into a tightly puckered hole. As her hand moved slowly closer, she began to shudder and her eyelids started to flicker. The cool, waxy stick was about to touch the center of the ring when she opened her eyes wide and saw Altstad. It could not have taken more than a tenth of a second for her mouth to open gapingly and for the scream 'RAAAAAAAPE' to break out of her throat. The sound hurt Altstad's eardrums, the shock almost knocked him over. The woman moved toward him quickly and menacingly. Her bags, the handgrips of which were tied together in series, followed her, scraping and scratching over the pavement. In confused terror, Altstad ran under the bridge, the woman in pursuit. Her scream repeated itself in a high-pitched caw that was echoed and amplified by the tunnel. 'RAAAAAAAAPE. RAAAAAAAAPE. RAAAAAAAAPE. RAAAAAAAAPE. RAAAAAAAAPE.'

Altstad ran out of the tunnel and kept running. A woman jogger coming from the right on the north-south path slowed down when she heard the scream, and stared at Altstad when she realized what she was hearing. Still in panic, all he could do was hunch his shoulders to project an image of ignorance and screw up his face in an attempt to say She's crazy. This did not reassure the woman on the path, but she did not stop Altstad from dashing past her.

Under the shower, Altstad struggled to figure out what was going on. His experiences of the morning refused to leave his mind, crowding it as if he was still seeing and feeling them directly. He wondered whether they had really happened, or if they had somehow entered his mind without having had to happen first. Gradually, they subsided to mere memories. The color and sound dimmed, the continuity was shredded, smell and touch vanished. By the time he climbed over the rim of the tub, he felt as if he was once more in charge of his mind.

He needed his mind for what he had to do in Houston that afternoon. When he arrived home the night before, there was a fax for him from the Reynolds. Henry Walker could see him at two o'clock. If he caught the ten-thirty flight out of La Guardia, the museum driver would pick him up at the airport. Altstad was dressed and putting the painting into a carrying case when the phone rang. He let the machine pick up.

'Goddamn it, Lodewijk, this is Mitchell. Why the fuck aren't you there? I have to speak to you right away. Call me the instant you get this message.'

Altstad had heard Fleishig talking to other people on the telephone like that during meetings at his office. This was the first time his prize customer had used the treatment on him. He could not say he liked it. He finished packing the Steen, slipped the *Kensington* proofs and his manuscript for it into a zipper compartment on the outside of the case, put on a raincoat and left his locked and barred apartment to look for a cab.

On the plane, he corrected the proofs.

Two halves of a whole: Jan Steen's *Wedding Night of Sarah and Tobias* reconstructed

Lodewijk Altstad

On November 20, 1672, a painting by Jan Steen (1626-

79) was pledged as security for a loan made to the Hague tavernkeeper Govert Spil by the Remonstrant clergyman Simon Greivanus. The transaction was recorded by notary Adriaen van Heusden, who described the painting as follows: 'Tobias and his bride giving thanks to the Lord for deliverance from the fearful demon.' (For the complete Dutch text and translation of the document, see Appendix A.) In this article, it is proposed that the painting referred to has survived, but that it was cut vertically into two fragments: *Tobias and his Bride* is the signed work acquired four years ago by the Reynolds Museum of Art in Houston, Texas, and the 'fearful demon' a newly discovered work here published for the first time.

Extreme prudence is called for in identifying existing works with mentions of the kind cited above. In this case, we believe the proposal stands up to scrutiny for three main reasons: 1. Jan Steen was known personally to all three parties involved in the transaction: Spil, his creditor Greivanus and notary van Heusden; 2. a painting of this subject appears in the catalogue of the auction sale of the estate of Greivanus's son and heir, with dimensions corresponding closely to the reconstructed whole; and 3. no other painting by Steen of the wedding night of Tobias and Sarah has ever emerged, either in documents or in the literature.

The first part of the present article advances arguments in support of the assumption that the two canvases were once a single work. Secondly, the iconography of the painting and its place in the oeuvre of Jan Steen are discussed. And in conclusion the historical evidence linking the reconstructed work to the document of 1672 is reviewed.

As usual, the proofs were a torment. Altstad was annoyed but not pained that the Dutch document was nothing but typos or that coding errors introduced Greek characters and mathematical symbols and left entire paragraphs in italics or small caps. What hurt were the insufficiencies he saw in every sentence of his writing. What until now he thought was a tightly argued and gracefully written piece of scholarship revealed itself in typesetting to be awkward, flawed by self-serving reasoning and incurably academic. But even after he read it a second time, as uncharitably as he could, it remained convincing.

The case of the dismembered Jan Steen was closed when he and Henry Walker put the two paintings side by side in the restoration department of the Reynolds. It was obvious at a glance that Altstad was right. The two fragments were the same height, and their combined width produced a landscape format of classical proportions. The picture space, the scale of the figures and the tonality interlocked seamlessly. To expel all doubt, the smoke rising from the incense dish on the left of the bridal chamber began forming a loop which came round to the right of the demon. After some two hundred and fifty years, Steen's composition returned to view.

The two men watched in silence as the life blood began circulating once more between the disjoined members. Tobias and Sarah knelt on a bare plank floor beside a canopied bed strewn with roses and daisies. They were dressed splendidly, Tobias in an olive velvet suit slashed at the elbows and knees, Sarah in a changeant pink and green dress of crinkly silk. His hands were folded piously, her arms spread in supplication. Both of them looked up with rapt and serious expressions.

Separated from them as yet by two frames, on the left, was the demon. Despite beak, feathers and talons, his build and posture were human. Bending forward to stay out of the smoke, he turned his head completely around to look back at Sarah.

'You know the story better than I do,' said Walker. 'How does it go again?'

'It's in my article,' Altstad said, looking for the place in the proofs. 'Tobias is on the road with the angel Raphael, disguised as a man named Azarias. They have caught a fish, and Tobias, on the instructions of the angel, has saved the heart, liver and gall. Then, as they approach the place Ecbatana, "the angel said to the young man, 'Brother, today we shall stay with Raguel. He is your relative, and he has an only daughter named Sarah. I will suggest that she be given to you in marriage, because you are entitled to her and to her inheritance, for you are her only eligible kinsman. The girl is also beautiful and sensible.' Then the young man said to the angel. 'Brother Azarias, I have heard that the girl has been given to seven husbands and that each died in the bridal chamber. Now I am the only son my father has, and I am afraid that if I go in I will die as those before me did, for a demon is in love with her, and he harms no one except those who approach her.

' "But the angel said to him, 'Now listen to me, brother, for she will become your wife; and do not worry about the demon, for this very night she will be given to you in marriage. When you enter the bridal chamber, you shall take live ashes of incense and lay upon them some of the heart and liver of the fish so as to make a smoke. Then the demon will smell it and flee away, and will never again return. And when you approach her, rise up, both of you, and cry out to the merciful God, and he will save you and have mercy on you. Do not be afraid, for she was destined to you from eternity.' " And that is what happened.'

'I never noticed it before, but as you were reading the story, I saw clearly that the two of them are frightened out of their wits. They are looking up not just to pray, but also to avoid the sight of the demon. That aspect of the painting was invisible if you didn't know the story, and if you didn't see the demon.'

'It works both ways. Without Sarah in the scene, the demon's expression looked purely evil. But now you can see that it is closer to despair. The demon is a tragic lover.'

Altstad's voice grew weaker as he spoke. His throat tightened, his lips drew back and his face went stiff. His eyes were riveted on the demon in horror. It was larger than a man, and much more powerful, with the unfeeling look of a bird of prey. Staring at its belly, Altstad noticed for the first time a detail that had been painted over: a long, raw, pointed erection, studded with barbs of hardened flesh. The demon had killed seven men in

Tobias's position, and now it wanted to rip, peck and fuck Sarah to pieces.

The picture space of the two canvases merged in Altstad's mind. He no longer saw the frames, and the bedroom opened up to him. Nothing but a thin cloud of foul smoke separated the demon from the praying figures. Where was the angel? Altstad was afraid to move or make another sound, but probably could not have done either had he wanted to. It was his fault that the demon had been brought back to torment and perhaps kill Tobias and Sarah. How could he have endangered the lives of those beautiful young people so thoughtlessly? He knew from his work on the article what the monster was after. How could he have done the one thing that threatened them after these centuries of peace: bringing the demon to the Reynolds. And what was to stop it from turning on Walker and himself? The angel said that the demon harmed no one but those who approached Sarah, but weren't they doing that with their staring and meddling? Altstad's genitals shrunk toward the safety of his pelvis, and his hands darted to cover them.

'Mr. Altstad, is anything wrong?'

Walker stepped between Altstad and the paintings to look the art dealer in the face. Seeing him, Altstad became aware simultaneously of his panic and the fact that it was gone.

'I'm sorry. I think I must be more tired than I realized. I'm fine.'

'Are you sure? We could take a break if you like. Can I get you something to drink?'

The emotion Altstad had felt a moment before had vanished completely, leaving behind it nothing but mild embarrassment.

'No, really, let's go on. This is too fascinating to interrupt.'

'Well, all right, but please do ask for tea or a drink whenever you feel like it. Shall we have a look at the backs?'

The *Wedding Night* had been relined at the Reynolds. An old relining canvas had been removed and the original canvas was now attached to a new one. The *Demon* had been pasted onto a thin wooden panel, probably in the nineteenth century. It would have to be removed before the two paintings could be rejoined. Comparison of the backs was unrevealing, and they turned the paintings around again. With a magnifying glass, Walker and Altstad examined the canvases near the edges. Garland-shaped cusps were visible along the tops, bottoms and outer edges, where the canvas had been tacked to the stretcher. The inner edges had no marks of that kind, indicating that the canvas had been cut there. A closer look at a spot where the paint was thin showed that an irregularity in the weave of the canvas, caused by a slack, unravelling thread, could be traced across the gap.

Altstad took notes for a postscript to his article. In addition to the corroborating evidence for his theory provided by the canvas and the satisfying visual impression of the whole, he was now able to report on the relative condition of the two works. The surface of the *Wedding Night* was flatter. As thinly as Jan Steen applied pigment, the paint layer was nonetheless visibly three-dimensional, with ridges along some brushstrokes and globs in the thickness of the shadows. Probably because of a hard-handed earlier relining, and perhaps exposure to corrosive air, the surface of the *Wedding Night* had lost its freshness. By comparison, the *Demon* was reasonably intact.

'Do you know that story about your painting when it was in Darling Hall? The money for that collection came from a coal mine. A lot of young women worked there at the mouth of the coal pit. One girl, crawling on all fours in a tunnel three feet high, would pull the loaded wagons of coal out of the pit. They would be tipped into a chute and a team of girls would clean the dirt off the coal as it tumbled past. These girls wore trousers, and every once in a while a reformer would get upset about this so-called social evil. That was a Victorian buzzword meaning sexual looseness. The House of Commons formed a committee to look into the matter and the mines did what they could to improve the moral image of their working girls. At the Darling Hall mine, Lord Warren introduced segregated lunchrooms for his male and female workers, and in the female lunchroom he hung the *Wedding Night*, from his own collection, with a poem in praise of the virgin bride. You can imagine what kind of remarks it must have drawn from girls who had to prove their fertility by bearing a child before any man would consider marrying them.

'Now that we can compare it to the *Demon*, I wonder whether the surface of the *Wedding Night* was affected by its hanging in a coal mine.'

Halfway through his story, Altstad realized that he was trouncing two of Molenaar's cardinal rules: Never Discuss the Morals of Moneymaking and Never Make a Disparaging Remark about a Painting in a Customer's Collection. In another situation, this might have cost him a sale. Now it had the beneficial effect of inspiring Walker to change the subject and get down to business.

'Well, Mr. Altstad, obviously we are interested in your painting. What price did you have in mind?'

'This is an exceptional situation. The painting is worth more to you than to anyone else. As a fragment, even now that it is an unquestionable Jan Steen, its value is limited. Nonetheless, I would like to offer it to you for the market price. The *Wedding Night*, I have heard, cost two-and-a-half million dollars. I can let you have the *Demon* for one million.'

This pretty speech could not be faulted, Walker thought, except for one thing. Two-and-a-half million dollars was a lot of money for a Jan Steen, and the Reynolds could have bought the *Wedding Night* for that amount even if it had been complete with demon. Today, they could probably have gotten it for a lot less. Having to pay a million to make the painting complete was just plain bad luck. Walker also doubted that Altstad could get anything like a million for the painting from anyone else. Unless there were someone out there to whom it was worth a million dollars to make the Reynolds look silly, or who would buy it and raise the price to two million. Still, the pressure to acquire the work was built into the situation, and would not go away as long as it was on the market. Better to take the damage now. The acquisition would generate terrific publicity, and create the kind of story that visitors would tell each other forever. He would have to go for it. But that was no reason to pay the dealer's price. He wasn't going to be running off with it to anyone else.

Walker used the self-suggestive trick he employed for price negotiations. He imagined that his wife had dragged him into a fancy jewelry store in the Galleria and asked the manager to show him a diamond bracelet. He had no intention of buying it for her, but rather than just walk away he allowed himself the fun of a cat-and-mouse game with the store, which was obviously on the verge of bankruptcy.

'One million dollars? That seems *very* high to me.'

It came out just right, making it sound as if Walker was not even going to start to think about a purchase until the price was cut at least by half.

Altstad got a sinking feeling in his stomach. He had overplayed his hand. This was not going to be the quick sale he needed. It was only a matter of time — days, a month at the most — before the Reynolds found out where the painting had come from and what he had paid for it.

'These are not the eighties anymore, Mr. Altstad. Houston is not the go-go town it used to be. Our donations are down dramatically, and we've had to lay off staff this past year.'

Walker was very pleased with himself. Now he made it sound as if the dealer had made an indecent proposition, as if his offer would aggravate unemployment in the Sunbelt.

Altstad downshifted abruptly.

'I'm sorry to hear that. When I named my price, I sincerely thought it was below the true value of a solid Jan Steen, and an amount that would pose no difficulty to a major institution such as the Reynolds.'

His ploy succeeded in bringing Walker back from the Galleria to the Museum. The Reynolds *was* a major institution, and it did have its pride. His acquisitions budget had not yet been affected by the recession, and it was getting harder to flush out really good European paintings. But he was damned if he was going to give up his advantage against this kid that easily.

'I understand,' he said in a sympathizing tone, leaving the

next move up to the opposition.

Trying to hide the depths of his despair, Altstad lowered the tone of the negotiations to what Molenaar called 'souk-in-the-kasbah' level.

'These are special circumstances, Mr. Walker. We are wedded to each other in this transaction in a unique way. So I will ask you a question that I would never normally pose. And that is simply this: what are you willing to pay?'

Walker was surprised at how easily it was going. The next move was practically mandatory: a round of dealer-dangling.

'I'm afraid I can't answer that question right now. I have to consult with my director and with our acquisitions committee. I'll need a little time.'

'There is no rush as far as I am concerned,' Altstad lied. 'I *could* give you a month. But I have to return the corrected proofs for my article in the *Kensington*, and if you will be buying the painting it would be nice to be able to publish it as a Reynolds acquisition. The article will be out in about a month, and by then I need an answer anyway.'

'When is your deadline for the proofs?'

'In a week,' Altstad lied again. A shorter period would reveal him to be up against the wall, as of course he was.

'I think I can manage that. I'll make a counter-offer within a week's time.'

Walker let Altstad use his phone to call Mitchell Fleishig. He was surprised when Fleishig himself answered. Usually he was put on hold for at least two full performances of 'California Dreaming'.

'Lodewijk, at last. Listen, something major is happening out here, and you are going to be in on it. A small group of us want to make a special donation of an important painting to a certain organization. I can't tell you more, but it's going to get into all the papers, and I'll make sure the art dealer who supplies us gets a big play. Am I in focus?'

'In a way.'

'Well, sharpen up a little, right? What we need is a painting by a name artist, of an easy, likeable subject, in good condition. The price range we are looking for is much higher than what I buy from you. Think on the order of two five, three mil. Dollars, not guilders. The only problem is time. We have to make a decision next week. The others wanted to go to Colnaghi or Wildenstein, but I told them no, I have a source with a much better price/quality ratio. So I want you to give me your best shot, Lodewijk. What can you get your hands on for us?'

'Never Sell Negative to an Eager Customer,' said Molenaar inside Altstad's head. Of course he had no stock in the price class Fleishig was talking about. But Molenaar did. He would cook up a deal with Molenaar, if Molenaar was still talking to him.

'I'm sure I can help you. There's an interesting possibility on my mind, but I have to have another good look before I put it on offer. I'll be back in Holland after the weekend, and I'll get straight to work on it.'

'No, that's too late. We have to move now. If I can't assure these people that we have a fair crack at a closing next week, they're going to go to London. Because you're calling me so goddamned late I've missed all of today's flights to Europe. But I'll be in Amsterdam Friday morning, and I want to see you there with the painting. You have a day on me.'

'It's not that simple, Mitchell. I'm calling from Houston, Texas, and I don't know if I can get to Amsterdam by tomorrow.'

'Houston, Texas. Terrific. Look, I'll hold and you find out if you can fly from Houston, fucking Texas, to Amsterdam this afternoon.'

Altstad put the horn down and went into the room next door. Within two minutes Walker's secretary booked him a seat on a flight from Houston to Amsterdam leaving at 5 pm.

'Mitchell? We're on. I'll pick you up at Schiphol on Friday morning. Just fax me your flight number.'

'Will do, Lodewijk. This is finally starting to shape up. There's only one more thing. Let's keep this to ourselves. Don't mention my name to anyone until we close, right?'

Fed, wined, belted and blanketed, Altstad tuned in to a program of cool jazz and closed his eyes. He was on board a KLM flight from Mexico City to Amsterdam via Houston. For the first time in his life, he was flying business class. It was empty enough so that all passengers travelling alone had a row to themselves. Behind the curtain, the economy section was jammed with Spanish-speaking tourists in cut-rate seats. The cabin crew in business class put on the airs of a maître d' in a private club, while their colleagues in economy ran around like monitors on an eighth-grade outing.

Flying business class for the first time in his life reminded him of the Plaza Hotel suicides you heard about. Washed-out people who treated themselves to a few days of luxury at the end and then let the poor chambermaid find their bodies.

He did not know what he would do if he lost his bet. But he knew what he was going to do now: raise to the limit. Why go to Molenaar with a three-million-dollar deal? He had a better idea.

Juliana Altstad owned an étage — the complete second story — of a row house in the part of Amsterdam known as Oud-Zuid, the Old South. It had never before occurred to her nephew, but while looking for a parking spot for the van he had borrowed from Molenaar, Altstad decided that the neighborhood had an antebellum quality. Extending west from the Museumplein and the Concertgebouw, it took for granted a certain level of culture not found elsewhere in Amsterdam. The long, straight, east-west streets were lined by big old row houses sinking into genteel decrepitude. Connecting them at intervals were short commercial blocks with specialty shops, bookstores, boutiques and restaurants which were no longer attracting their share of business from other neighborhoods or from the center. Oud-Zuid was awaiting a generation of Dutch Snopeses to sweep out the cobwebs and put a price tag on the culture. But first the war would have to be worked through. The war, in Oud-Zuid, was the Second World War, the indigestible products of which still blocked the metabolism of the neighborhood.

The mantelpiece in Juliana's living room and the lid of her grand piano were covered, as in many Dutch households, with family photographs. She and her five brothers and sisters, their parents and grandparents, one great-grandfather, four uncles and aunts, all married and with twelve children between them. In 1941 her mother's father had died. The next year, the three youngest children, Juliana and two boys, were sent to hide out from the Germans and their Dutch collaborators on a farm in Gelderland. The farmer kept the Jewish children locked in a feed loft for three years, letting them out only when there was mist and on rainy evenings. They survived the war; the other twenty-nine did not. Their unspeakable deaths made holy relics of Juliana's photographs.

Her brother Leo married unexpectedly in the late 1950s, fathered Lodewijk, and died. Juliana did not get along with her sister-in-law. Her brother Solly was still alive. He lived in the clinic for the demented at the end of the Valeriusstraat. They tottered him over to Juliana on Tuesday and Saturday for tea and a conversation which had found its form years before. Solly made her whisper so the neighbors could not hear. The only other relative who ever visited Juliana was Lodewijk.

'Don't kiss me,' she greeted her nephew. 'I have a strange cough. Why didn't you give me more warning? You always come at the wrong time.'

'I'm sorry, Tante Juul.' As hard as he tried to prepare for these visits, Juliana was always able to wound him. He was impressed by her speed this time around.

'So now you want the de Witte? Well, I'm not sure I want to sell. It's a very valuable painting, you know.'

'Yes, I know. That's why I waited all this time before asking. You do remember that when I started off in art dealing you told me I could sell it for you whenever I wanted to. Well, I waited until I was ripe to get the best deal for you. And now I am.'

'The best deal for me? Don't be such a hypocrite. You know you inherit everything anyway. What difference does it make to me how much you get for it? Do you really think you're already good enough to know what it's worth?'

Underneath it all, Altstad told himself, she was concerned about him. She just had her own miserable way of expressing it.

'Yes, I think I am. And I have a buyer ready to pay a good price.'

'Is it a Dutch museum?'

'No, it's a private collector in America.'

'That means I would never see the painting again. I have seen it practically every day of my life except when I was hidden. It was one of the things I missed the most.'

'All right, Tante Juul, I'll leave it here.'

'Did I say that? How nasty you can be, Lo. Sometimes I think you take more after your mother than your father. How is she, by the way?'

'Fine.'

'Do you know this collector?'

'Yes. He's my best customer.'

'But you sell cheap paintings. How can he pay for an expensive painting?'

'He isn't buying it alone. It's a group. They want to donate it. Maybe to a museum. He didn't say.'

'Why can't you give me a straight story? First it's a collector, then it's a group, now it's a museum. Do you know what's happening to the painting or don't you?'

'I know the man. He is building up a collection of Utrecht paintings. He's very serious about it. He reads everything that comes out. If he is organizing this purchase, I'm sure the painting is going to a worthwhile destination.'

Altstad knew that if his aunt laid eyes on Mitchell Fleishig, he could forget about the sale. She had never been to America, but she knew she didn't like it. Fleishig was the living embodiment of Aunt Juliana's worst prejudices against Americans. He was not exactly lying to his aunt, but he might as well have been.

'How can you be sure he's going to pay you once he has the painting?'

'He always has paid me until now. Anyway, that's the way art dealers do business. Auction houses ask for payment before delivery, but dealers don't. It's a matter of trust.'

'My father had trust. All I trust people for is to behave as selfishly as possible.'

Altstad knew better than to stand up for human nature in a discussion with Juliana.

'How soon do you want to take it?'

'Actually, I wanted to take it now. The customer is flying in from Los Angeles tomorrow to see it, and I want to get it cleaned and varnished first.'

'As usual, I am the last one to know. Obviously, you've made all your plans already without bothering to ask me. Why ask now? Go ahead, take it.'

'It isn't just a question of me taking it, Tante Juul. It's your property, and in order for me to sell it we have to have a formal agreement. I made up a consignment contract, in which I get a commission of 50% on the sale. I hope you remember that you told me we would split the proceeds of a sale fifty-fifty.'

'Of course I remember. But why does everybody else always remember what I promise them and never what they promise me?'

'Did I break a promise?'

'You're going to. You promised to go to the piano series in the Concertgebouw with me whenever you were in the country. Tomorrow Cherkassky is playing Chopin and Brahms, but you're going to be busy with your American customer. You know how much I love opus 117. Do you remember when I was teaching it to you? We heard Gilels play it and we couldn't talk about anything else for a month. We hadn't realized before how important the dynamics were. Everybody else fudges them or does just what they feel like. What a difference it makes when you play loud and soft as accurately as you play the notes and the tempi. Whenever I play those Intermezzi I think of Gilels and you. You were on my right, sitting straight up with your mouth open. I play them often. Cherkassky is ten years older than poor Gilels. Wouldn't it be wonderful to go together to hear how he plays them?'

'Of course it would. I would love nothing more. But you're right, I may have to go out with the customer. Maybe he'll be too tired for dinner and will want to go to bed early. But I can't promise, and if I don't show up, you'll be alone. Don't you think it would be better to invite someone else?'

'No. Here's your ticket. If you don't come, I'll leave the seat to my right empty and think of you. Take care of your business, Lo. And take care of yourself. You look terrible.'

*

Mitchell Fleishig's taste in color was not the same as Juliana Altstad's. As far as she was concerned, a good Dutch painting had a Rembrandtesque chiaroscuro and that was that. Her de Witte interior of the Portuguese synagogue came close enough. Beams of sunlight shining through the large south windows fell directly on one side of the large smooth columns, the intervening areas of the north inside wall and the floor in the foreground. Daylight showed through the five tall, rounded windows in the east wall, the smaller square windows above them and the round one in the semicircular wall closing the great barrel vault above the nave. The rest of the interior was in shadow. Because Juliana never had the painting cleaned, its yellowing varnish colored the painting sunset gold and crepuscular brown and gray. A man seen from the back, in a blue cloak with red collars and cuffs, stood out from the crowd. The other figures and the furnishings of the synagogue — the famous jacaranda Ark of the Covenant, the bema, the railings and benches — formed a closed, dark mass weighing down the center of the composition.

Juliana belonged to the Spinoza Lecture Society of Oud-Zuid, and she never missed the evenings when art historians spoke. She had heard all the famous professors from the art history institute of the University of Amsterdam. They confirmed what she felt: that great artists were not interested in *petite histoire*, picturesque details or decoration. They were after the fundamentals of design, pure space and the essence of light and dark. Johannes Haffner had shown them that if you squinted at Vermeer you would see Mondriaan. De Witte, like Rembrandt, was more like Mondriaan's antipode in modern art, Mark Rothko. Even the main subjects of their paintings, let alone the architectural backgrounds, were a mere pretext for experiments in form and light. Those were the means by which an artist communicated what he learned from a life dedicated to intense visual experience. By learning to look at their paintings in that way, you could develop a more profound relation to reality, like Haffner's.

That was not what Mitchell Fleishig was looking for in a painting. He was a follower of the West Coast guru of Dutch art, Ayn Morosov. She too taught that the subjects of Dutch paintings were a pretext for the artists. Subjects were for the garrulous Italians, who could never stop talking even while they painted. What the Dutch were after was a one-to-one visual relation with nature. The best of them came closer to it than anyone else before or since. And the greatest of them all, Rembrandt, used his gift to impose on the world a new scale of values, based on the bottom line of artistic creation. Rembrandt had the genius to convert raw experience into a marketable commodity. The only materials he needed were excrement-like pigments. Who could teach a man like that anything about nature or humanity, let alone art? Fleishig had once told Altstad in awe that tapes of Morosov's classroom lectures were used in New Age personality development courses for managers. All of them wanted to become instruments for converting dreck into gold.

This translated into a different aesthetic than Aunt Juliana's. What Fleishig looked for in a Dutch painting was lots of color, light and detail. He pored in rapture over the nearly microscopic image of the artist at the easel reflected on a carafe in a still life by de Heem that Altstad had sold him. The way the artist reduced himself that way to his proper place in the continuum while taking the whole universe in a tiny reflection with him wiped Fleishig out. If he could merge with the L.A. ambience as organically as de Heem had become part of his scene, then he could influence the picture from the inside. To achieve that degree of hyper-effectiveness you had to free yourself completely of self-delusion and become a master of illusion. You could do it by prestidigitation, and earn easy millions. But if you were after billions, as Fleishig was, he confided to Altstad, you needed art. He wanted to see exactly how the Dutch painters did it, down to the last brushstroke.

For the art dealer, this was no problem. The de Witte lent itself just as readily to Fleishig's prejudices as to Aunt Juliana's. Paper is patient, says the Dutch proverb. So is paint. Although he had never seen the painting cleaner than it was now, he knew what was beneath the varnish. The Portuguese synagogue was dedicated in 1675, and de Witte had not painted it until about five years later. In earlier decades, the artist had been fond of complicated angles, impenetrable shadows set off by oversaturated colors, unreadable spaces and *trompe l'oeil* effects. But by the late seventies, he had cooled down. His compositions had become simplified, and he condescended to pay at least token heed to the rules of linear perspective. When the Rijksmuseum cleaned its synagogue painting, it turned out to be suffused with bright, even light and marked by rhythmic color accents of nearly pastel delicacy. Altstad knew that Aunt Juliana's version would clean up the same way. Fleishig would be delighted by the light red curtains drawn back from all the windows and the three-tiered chandeliers, with their hundreds of snuffed candles. It was too much to hope that the reflections on the brass balls would include a diminutive draftsman, but you never knew. The colors and cut of the costumes would emerge, and you would be able to see the prayer shawls that the men and boys wore over their broad-brimmed hats. All it took to postmodernize the de Witte for Fleishig was a pot of solvent.

The painting restorer who did all of Altstad's work lived in the Koestraat, a few blocks from his own place and from the Portuguese synagogue. He parked illegally in front of her door and the two of them carried the canvas into Ineke van der Heyden's studio. On an easel, under strong lamps, Altstad was able to see well for the first time a painting he had known all his life. He was as nervous as he always was studying a painting after acquiring it or taking responsibility for selling it. There were so many ways to deceive yourself. A Belgian art conservationist had built a ladder of fifteen steps between a complete fake and a completely original painting. Even that chart simplified the situation: complete originality does not exist even in new art, let alone in three-hundred-and-fifty-year-old hostages to time. Despite this, few people in the art world could keep themselves from forming a quick, strong opinion about the authenticity and quality of a work they saw for the first time. An art dealer had to trust this judgment and mistrust it at the same time. Altstad was relieved that the de Witte did not collapse immediately under hard scrutiny. The composition was definitely invented by Emanuel de Witte, and the canvas was definitely painted in the seventeenth century. That still did not make it a class A original; it could be a contemporary copy. The signature *E. De Witte* looked good, and so did the date, of which the last two digits were missing. A signature was another of those signs which need not mean anything, but which nonetheless always contributed to one's faith in authenticity. The condition of the surface was reasonable. His gut reaction told Altstad that the painting was authentic, and just as interesting as the three published versions of the subject. There was no reason not to ask a de Witte price for the painting. To ask less would mean that the seller was discounting doubts.

'There isn't much I can do in one day, Lodewijk. You know that.'

'Of course. All I want is a dusting and varnish removal in two or three areas. The signature, of course. And then, let's see. How about two of the windows on the right and these figures in black. That way you get an idea of the color in the light areas and the gorgeous depth of the blacks. Remember, it's to show to a customer. Give it the before-and-after look.'

'Do we know anything about de Witte's ideas of color?'

'As usual, what we know is a bunch of contradictions. Between the fifties and the eighties he definitely moved to a lighter, more colorful palette. But then there's a story in Houbraken that gives a very different idea. De Witte hated Gerard de Lairesse, and he once insulted him by saying that his paintings looked like the Prince's flag. *Oranje, blanje, bleu*: orange, white and blue, just like the colors we're about to bring back to view. Go figure it. And let's be honest with ourselves. If we were treating the painting for my Aunt Juliana, we would not remove all the old varnish, and we would give it back to her with that traditional de Witte look. Now that it's on offer to a younger buyer, who likes clarity and color, we'll go right down to the pigment and bring out as many local tones as we can find. I don't see anything wrong with that, do you?'

Ineke didn't.

Altstad did not get home until late in the afternoon. He had gone straight from Schiphol to Molenaar's gallery on the Rokin for a midday debriefing over sherry and *broodjes*. For the first time, he held out on Molenaar. He told him about the auction and the Jan Steen but not about Fleishig. From there he went to Tante Juul and Ineke van der Heyden and then dropped off Molenaar's van before walking home to the Kromboomssloot. Surprised by the smallness of the pile of mail for him on the table in the hallway, he realized with even more surprise that there had only been four deliveries since he left for the airport on Sunday.

His apartment, like Katy's, was a new unit built into an old house — a seventeenth-century warehouse in Altstad's case. The floor surface of the two studio apartments was about the same, but because the Dutch have smaller closets, bathrooms and vestibules, his seemed larger. It lay on a small canal dug in the sixteenth century to service the ropeyard of Cornelis Pietersz Boom, an outspoken Calvinist in a city still run by Catholics. He, his forefathers and descendants occupied positions of power in Amsterdam for two hundred years. Say what you like about them, Altstad sometimes heard himself arguing, the Calvinists let the Jews settle here and become their neighbors. His own family had lived in Amsterdam for over two hundred years. Why should he sometimes feel like a stranger here?

He had nothing with him but the shoulder bag which he had taken to Houston for what he thought was a quick round trip. All it contained were some newspapers, KLM's business-class giveaway, his pocket diary and his article for the *Kensington*. Having faxed the corrected proofs to London from Molenaar's, complete with the big lie that the Reynolds had acquired the second half of Jan Steen's *Tobias and Sarah*, there was nothing between him and a shower, a change of clothes, a drink, a lonesome meal at the reading table of the Engelbewaarder, where he could catch up on the week's news, and a long night's sleep. Fleishig's plane didn't get in from Los Angeles until a quarter to eleven the next morning.

Altstad was well into the preliminaries of this delightful evening when he was stopped in his tracks by the sight of a painting of a girl on his bedroom wall. Without taking his eyes from it, he walked toward it, lifted it off the wall and brought it to a standing lamp in his living room. Holding it under the light, he looked at it closely and heard himself mutter 'Original. Amsterdam.'

This time, he was able to break the spell himself. He put the painting on the ground facing the wall, took a bottle of Hoegaarden out of the refrigerator and cut a wedge out of a lemon in his fruit bowl. He poured the Belgian *bière blanche* into a tall glass, dropped the lemon in and settled into his reading chair. My mind is snapping, he thought. If I lose it, I wonder what form my madness will take. Sex? Money? Dementia? Please, not fear.

Lodewijk's neighborhood was not like his Aunt Juliana's. Although it was a lot older, there were no cobwebs here. They had been blown away in the Nieuwmarkt Urban Renewal Project and the battles to which it gave rise. In a clean-up frenzy, the municipality had decided to take advantage of the metro excavations to renovate the rundown area between the Waalseilandsgracht and the Oude Schans. Bordering on the old, devastated Jewish quarter, a seedy new Chinatown and the eternal red-light district, the Nieuwmarkt area had suffered badly from the depression, the war, and the postwar years of austerity. In the 1960s it housed a mixed population of underearners: workers in defunct crafts, the moms and pops of marginal family businesses, students, the chronic unemployed, small-time dealers in palliative substances and services, other minor criminals, and the unfortunate shopkeepers who catered to their trade. No one had realized that these people thought of themselves as a neighborhood until the wreckers went to work. The inhabitants had seen the excesses of soullessness of which the township was capable in the infamous Maupoleum on the nearby Jodenbreestraat — four hundred running meters of cheap concrete module where thirty seventeenth-century houses had once stood, on a site Rembrandt would have seen from his front door had a merciful Providence not driven him bankrupt, forcing him to move crosstown, and then carried him off with three hundred years to spare.

The first demolitions on the Nieuwmarkt touched an exposed nerve, and the painful struggle was on. The Dutch Maoist youth fought the Amsterdam authorities as if they were the Vietcong taking on the American Army. They succeeded well enough to save the Nieuwmarkt from wall-to-wall renovation. It ended up as a self-conscious blend of old, fake-old, new-bowing-to-old, middle-aged utilitarian and provocative vacancy. Every house and every inhabitant had been through a purge. The survivors were left with lingering doubts as to whether it was all worth it.

The greatest survivor of all stood alone in the middle of the New Market Square itself: the Weighing Hall. Built in 1488 as Amsterdam's gate to the east, the gorgeous brick hulk lost this function in 1617, when a new extension brought it within the city walls. Since then it had served not only as a weighing hall but also housed half a dozen guilds and as many museums. At various times, it was used by the university, the fire department and the municipal archives. After the departure of the Jewish Historical Museum in 1986, the building became an emblem of the mix of indecisiveness and overcompensation that is a trademark of the Amsterdam town government. In a misplaced piece of business as usual that will go down in the annals of bureaucratic vandalism, the township decided that the upkeep of their unique five-hundred-year old monument of civic architecture would have to be paid for by the open market. They turned the building over to a new club for people in banking and communications, which ripped out the insides to make way for a café-restaurant by a French designer who was so busy that he did his creative work on flights to and from Japan. As this plan ran its rocky course toward bankruptcy and beyond, the deterioration of the building proceeded at an accelerated tempo. Altstad looked at the Weighing Hall commiseratingly on his way to the Kloveniersburgwal, in an attempt to drive the future out of his mind with the past. But there was no past, only the tottering, punchdrunk, patched-up remains of a big, unhandy relic.

Literair Café De Engelbewaarder, the Guardian Angel, had a history that followed the waves of social geography of the neighborhood. Journalists, writers and the better kind of bum hung out there in the seventies, a fickle public which by the late eighties had abandoned it to alcoholics on welfare. It was now sufficiently regentrified for Altstad's not overfastidious taste. He nodded at some acquaintances, sat down at the reading table with his back to the door and went through the new weeklies over entrecôte and some glasses of the house Provence red.

Mitchell Fleishig stood speechless in front of the easel, breathing in irregular gulps. He had not slept on the plane, and had spent the eleven-hour flight in growing fear of being recognized. Benny Santangelo would not like the idea that he was flying to Europe. He had not told anyone, not even Beatrice. If they made her talk, it was better for both of them that she believe he was in Palm Springs trying to raise money. Benny's men would probably think he was with a girlfriend. Maybe Beatrice would too. All the better.

Once he was on board, he began to worry that Santangelo might be monitoring the passenger lists on flights out of LAX. He had no idea how to get a false passport, and was flying under his own name. He had paid for his ticket with a credit card that Santangelo would have no trouble tracing. The cabin crew could have been tipped to watch out for him, he might be spotted by someone he knew. In Amsterdam he had to do something dangerous he had never done before. And he would have to look Altstad in the eye. He liked Altstad. By the time he landed he was half sick with anxiety, guilt and exhaustion.

Altstad and Ineke van der Heyden stood a few feet behind him, waiting for his reaction to the Emanuel de Witte. He wanted to make the right sounds, but he was having trouble even focusing on the painting. The first thing he saw were the figures of a father and son in prayer shawls. His gulps started turning into sobs. He caught himself, swallowed, turned away and walked around the room, rubbing his eyes.

'Amazing picture,' he managed to get out. 'Wonderful. Very moving.'

Altstad was astonished to see Fleishig respond so emotionally to a painting. Apparently, he had been misjudging his customer.

Maybe he hadn't been showing him the right paintings. He looked for a way to help him over his minor collapse.

'Shall I tell you about the cleaning?'

'Yes, yes. Tell me about the cleaning.'

'I asked Ineke to treat a few sample areas so we could get an idea of how the painting will look after a proper cleaning. Ineke, what did you do exactly?'

'All I did was to swab those areas with a very dilute synthetic solvent and turpentine. I saved the used swabs for you, so you can see I only took off varnish, and probably not even all of it. But still, you can see how bright the colors are. It should clean up very nicely. I also looked over the rest of the surface. There's a little rubbing, and I think some of the highlights have been touched up. But on the whole the paint layer is in very good condition, and so is the canvas.'

Fleishig was regaining control of himself.

'That's just wonderful. I think this is exactly what we are looking for. Is there any problem with the attribution?'

'The painting has never been questioned, and it's in the standard literature. There are three other views by de Witte of the synagogue, one in the Rijksmuseum, one in the Israel Museum and one that disappeared from Berlin in the war. De Witte usually did more than one version of a successful view. Because the painting is typical and part of the accepted oeuvre, it has the inertia of middle-of-the-road art-historical opinion going for it. That's worth a lot. I also asked Ineke to check the signature. It looks characteristic and seems to have been painted wet-in-wet.'

Altstad's mental Molenaar kicked him in the shins. He was being too defensive — Molenaar would call it nihilistic. Authenticity proves itself. Talk about inimitable quality, technique whose secret went to the grave with the last Golden Age master, atmosphere you can cut with a knife, and the human warmth so sadly missing in the art of our own cynical century. Whatever you do, don't talk scholarly consensus about authenticity unless it's unavoidable. Somewhere out there,

there's always some schmuck of an art historian with doubts.'

'That's good to hear. I definitely think this is for us. I didn't tell you before, but the donation is in honor of a Jewish cause. So the painting could not be better. This painter really must have loved the Jews.'

Altstad gave his mental Molenaar a wise-guy grin.

'If he did, they were all he did love. De Witte is the most famous misanthrope in the history of Dutch art. Houbraken called him a stranger in his own country, with a knack for turning friends into enemies. He tells a little anecdote I wish I could forget. A young painter who admired de Witte once showed him his work for criticism. De Witte glanced at it and said 'You must be a happy man, if you can satisfy yourself making this kind of crap.' He must have been envious of the young man. He himself was unable to find contentment of any kind. Come to think of it, he reminds me of an anthropologist I once met. Anyway, de Witte lost all his patrons, after trying to cheat the widow of a man who had kept him alive for a few years. He borrowed an old painting of his own from her, and then tried to return a new copy. He reminds me of Gulley Jimson — did you ever read *The Horse's Mouth*? But less lovable. When I read things like that about artists I admire, I always think that if they had me as a friend, things would have turned out different. I would have understood them and they would have been able to turn to me when things got bad. But that's romantic nonsense. When I was in school I worked as a volunteer in a mental clinic, and I found out that the patients were there for very good reasons. Anyway, after one last fight with his last landlord, de Witte tried to hang himself from the public latrine on a bridge and fell into the water and drowned. That night the canals froze over, and his body wasn't found until the thaw, eleven weeks later.'

'That's terrible, just terrible. But the man could not have been all bad. Just look at the way he shows a Jewish congregation. You can't do that without feeling sympathy for the Jews. You can practically feel the bonding. Maybe he couldn't get along with people, but he must have been very religious.'

'He was the first to deny it. He used to say that at the age of fifteen the scales fell from his eyes. After that he took particular pleasure in pestering believers about the Bible.'

Enough is enough, Altstad thought. He threw Fleishig a bone.

'At a deeper psychological level, though, you are very right. De Witte must have been starved for a feeling of community. He must have felt like the prodigal son, dreaming about being reconciled with his people.'

Fleishig pursed his lips, narrowed his eyes and nodded, to indicate that he was receiving the message in all its profundity. This was the stuff he wanted to hear. Altstad sacrificed himself to the cause and ladled up some balm.

'What you see in his paintings is the wholeness of the community from which he shut himself out. As an outsider in his own culture, he knew the meaning of belonging even better than the regular worshippers. Perhaps he was able to depict Jews so warmly because they were the Old People despised by the Christians. So there are two levels of rejection and acceptance in the painting: the Christian-Jewish relationship and that of the artist and his culture. Your response to the painting shows that you have an instinctive sensitivity to this.'

Hoe krijg je het over je lippen?, he asked himself. Where do you get the bloody nerve? And all for a lousy two million dollars.

'That's a wonderful analysis, Lodewijk. I think that opens the painting right up. That says it all. The only thing left to talk about is price. Let's not go into that now. I don't want to defile this moment by talking about money. And I'm also too tired. Can you take me to my hotel now? We'll get together for drinks and dinner this evening.'

Altstad picked up Fleishig's overnight bag. Both men thanked Ineke and left. They walked the short distance to the new hotel on the Old Side where Fleishig was staying.

*

Fleishig did not take the nap he said he needed. After watching Altstad turn the corner of the Kloveniersburgwal from the window of his room, he put on his coat again and left the hotel. He wandered around until he came across a telephone booth. There he dialed a local number he had gotten from Blackbeard.

16 / Amsterdam, Friday evening

At seven o'clock the Friday evening crowd in the men's sauna of Fleishig's hotel, soaked in sweat and alcohol, was producing as much hot air as the Swedish furnace. The option traders, advertising executives and commercial TV producers opened their ventilation valves all the way to let off the pressure of the week. Whatever winding down this accomplished was more than offset by the strain of holding in their bellies, flaunting or hiding their genitals as the case dictated, and pretending to be at ease with each other's nakedness. They shouted in high pitch about deals and soccer.

Altstad, who had never been to a sauna before, was curious enough not to make Fleishig insist more than once that they take their drinks there. He followed his customer through a cycle of hot room, cold plunge, hot room and shower before they settled down in deck chairs under lointowels with beers from the tap. He could look at Fleishig now without the effort of not reacting to the excessive bulk he carried around in unhandy pockets of drooping flesh on his breasts, belly and bottom. His own body deviated in the opposite direction from the ideal that haunted the sauna like a ghost you could see only in the corner of your eyes. He was skin and bones, as his mother used to say. 'Fat and skinny had a race, Fat fell down and broke his face.' Katy's little nephew had chanted that at him and then cracked up laughing, unable to go on. Altstad wondered who won.

Altstad knew some of the other visitors. The entire junior staff of the Amsterdam office of Old York seemed to be there. Had he chanced on a hidden node where the art market intersected the economy? Would it help his career if he spent more time in the sauna and less at the National Center for Art History?

Fleishig looked straight ahead, speaking just loudly enough to be heard.

'Tell me, Lodewijk, what kind of prices has de Witte been fetching at auction?'

They were getting to the tricky part. Although Aunt Juliana's painting was valuable, it was not really in the price class Fleishig was looking for. But it wasn't just a price class Fleishig needed. He needed a good, likeable old master and he needed it now. Altstad had one, and there was no reason to let it go for less than Fleishig was willing to pay. Having raised the stakes on his bet to the limit, he was now going to bluff.

'That's just it. There hasn't been a de Witte of this importance on the block for a long time. I would place a de Witte like ours between the Berckheyde level of about one million and the Saenredam level of six. This painting also has the subject going for it. The fantasy pieces, where he mixes architecture from different buildings, aren't as interesting. A good painting of the New Church in Delft or the Old Church in Amsterdam is worth a lot more. There are terrific examples of both in LA, as you know. But the Portuguese synagogue is the rarest and is probably the subject that appeals most to the market right now. Certainly in America. Forgive my cynicism, but you know as well as I do that even if the museum directors are still wasps, most of the trustees and benefactors are Jewish.'

'And for this we have to pay, right? From one Jewboy to another, Lodewijk, you should be charging me a premium for a shul?'

'That's the snoga, Mitchell, slang for esnoga. The Portuguese Jews don't speak Yiddish. And who said I was charging you a premium? The thought would not have crossed my mind.'

'So what is your thought?'

'Three and a half.'

Fleishig finished his beer and signalled for two more.

'Who does the painting belong to?'

'As it happens, my own aunt. But she has signed a consignment agreement. I'm free to sell it at my discretion.'

'Did you talk price with her?'

'No. I didn't want to make her nervous with such big numbers.'

'The situation is such that I am not in a position to agree with you on a price. There's a group of us, and the others have given me until Monday morning to come up with a proposal. Personally, I am convinced that when they see this painting they will ankle. But will they know enough to realize that it is worth three and a half? That's what I'll have to sell to them. I think I have a good chance.'

'I've never seen you sell, but I know how you negotiate when you buy, and I have always been very impressed. I'm sure you can sell the painting better than I could.'

'If these people were art professionals, I would take you along for the negotiations. But they wouldn't even know what kind of questions to ask, let alone understand your answers. I think I know how to get to them. But I need a margin to work with. When they start to weaken, I have to nail it to them quick. And that you do with price.'

'Yes, of course. But in this case I have no reason to lower it by much. I think this painting is very saleable at three five, I want to get the best price I can for my aunt, and I'm in no rush. Still, you are my best customer, and I would really like to sell the painting through you. And since you are bringing in the deal, I can offer you a commission. So I'll tell you what. I'll give you a ten percent commission. If you have to drop the price to make the sale, take it out of that. If you don't, keep it.'

'That's very decent of you, Lodewijk.'

'I just want you to promise me one thing. If the sale collapses, the entire matter has to be kept forever confidential. This painting is completely fresh to the market, and I want to keep it that way. I don't want *anyone* to know that it was on offer and turned down, at any price at all.' Especially not Willem Molenaar, Altstad thought.

'That's fine with me. I'll make them give me their personal pledge on the matter. No, I'll go further. They don't even know where the painting is coming from or where I am now. Suppose I tell them that it's from a dealer in . . . say Palm Springs, California? That way, even if it got out that a de Witte painting of the Amsterdam synagogue was on offer — which these people are not likely to remember — you can always say that it wasn't your painting.'

'That would be wonderful. I really appreciate it.'

'No problem. If anyone asks you if you know where I am this weekend, just say I called you for advice from Palm Springs. If we close the sale and make the donation, of course I'll give you a big play. But if it doesn't go through, you'll never be mentioned.'

After eight o'clock, the weekend changed phase and the noise level in the sauna fell off. Fleishig excused himself and Altstad had a better look around. The groups had dwindled to a few pairs of conversation partners, speaking more quietly and earnestly now. They were letting their hair down, he thought. The ones with no place to go had woman problems. They were complaining to each other that their wives didn't understand why they had to have girlfriends. He missed Katy.

Fleishig came back and suggested one more turn in the hot room. They sat down and took in the other schwitzers: two men, each on his own. These were not social saunagoers. A superannuated beach bum with an all-over tan and gold dangling from wrist, ankle and neck, with more flab on one bicep than the other had on his whole built-up body. These were men who fetishized the flesh.

'Shut the door!' Altstad heard the beach bum say. The man on the threshold didn't know the drill. He mumbled 'Pardún,' entered the sauna and turned a snow-white ass to the company as he figured out how to close the wooden latch. His pasty whiteness extended across his entire body, under a cover of thick black hair, up to his wrists and neck. A ring as sharp as a tonsure separated his blackened face from his blanched scalp. His hands and face were dark not from a transient tan, but more as if they had been tattooed by the sun. He had the coloration of a peasant, Altstad thought, or a worker from a country where people kept on all their clothing in the sun. Altstad was surprised that social differences could show up so clearly even in the raw. It bothered him to find himself wondering what the man was doing there. His self-consciousness increased when the man climbed to the high shelf opposite Fleishig and Altstad and began peering at them.

'Whenever you're ready,' Fleishig said. 'I don't want to make a late night of it.'

They put on the hotel bathrobes they had left in a locker and took a back elevator to Fleishig's room, where they had changed. To Altstad's surprise, Fleishig called room service for a dinner he had ordered in advance; a waitress rolled it in and set it up. On Fleishig's previous visits to Amsterdam, he had always pressed Altstad into taking him to the newest restaurant.

'I ordered a cold fish buffet for the two of us. I hope that's all right with you.'

When the waitress lit the candles, Altstad made a joke about the Sabbath queen who visited Jews on Friday night when they said the blessing over the Sabbath flame.

One of the wine coolers steamed with a bottle of aquavit on dry ice. Fleishig poured big drinks, unveiled a bowl of black caviar with blinis and cream, and raised his glass.

'Gut shabbas, Lodewijk. Le . . ., le . . .' He choked and coughed, shaking his head violently.

Altstad waited for the attack to subside and finished the toast himself.

'Le'chaim.'

After lunch, Altstad drove Fleishig and the de Witte, in a carrying case, to Schiphol. They shook hands at the gate to passport control.

'Thanks for everything, Lodewijk. You'll hear from me on Monday. Don't forget the photo.'

Altstad had promised tò fax Fleishig a photograph of the interior of the Portuguese synagogue taken from the spot where de Witte had made his view. Visual comparisons of that kind are always intriguing, and although an aesthetic theory of artistic worth would deny that they affect the value of a work, they do.

The brass plate on the door read LEO ALTSTAD. Leo had died more than twenty-five years earlier, and his widow had moved twice since. The plate moved with her. Lily Altstad-de Vries would not think of replacing his name with hers. That would be like removing Leo's grave, as if he had never lived and died. Occasionally, the name on the door gave rise to a misunderstanding, and someone would ask for Mr. Altstad. Without resentment, she would sigh deeply and say 'Ach, my poor husband is no longer with us,' and her eyes would fill with tears. If the visitor expressed regrets, she would sob and say, 'What can you or I do about it? *God beschikt*. It was God's decision.'

She had never felt closer to Leo than in the months after his death. She had him all to herself then. Misunderstandings over the door plate brought that time back. They let her mourn for him again, and left her feeling sad but peaceful.

Lodewijk was two years old when his father died. He was not sure whether he remembered him or not. His visual image of his father looked so much like the family photographs that he doubted his own recollections. There was one memory he thought might be authentic. He was sitting in a stroller watching construction work on the RAI, the giant convention hall for the annual automobile show. His father stood behind him. A small power shovel was making its way toward them, digging its teeth into the ground and dropping loads of earth to one side. Every time the shovel hit the ground, his father said, '*Hap, jongen,*' — Bite into it, boy — just as he did when he fed Lootje. Lodewijk got scared and started to cry. His father picked him up and hugged him. His breath and body smelled sour.

Once he had told this to Jan Mark Rigter, who smiled condescendingly and told him it was a typical screen memory.

'Do you remember the next time you saw a power shovel?' he asked. The answer popped into Altstad's mind at once, to his own surprise.

'Yes, I caught sight of one behind a shed at the cemetery when I was visiting my father's grave.'

'There you are. The unconscious is not very particular about chronology. What you think is a memory of your father is an Oedipal fantasy, from long after his death. You are symbolically eating him alive.' Altstad didn't believe him, but his faith in the accuracy of his memory was undermined.

Altstad's mother now lived *één hoog* — one floor up — in an Amsterdam schoolhouse in the Rivierenbuurt, the River District. It was a part of New South, below Old South, whose main streets are named for the rivers of the lowlands. The building was seventy years old, but was still owned and maintained, like a thousand others in the neighborhood, by the non-profit housing corporation which had built it. All were in the same red brick, with yellow-white woodwork. No apartment was vacant, none overcrowded. By putting some of the best Dutch architects of their day to work on apartments and small houses for workers and shop-owners, and by keeping them to budget, the corporations had succeeded in creating neighborhoods which never went out of fashion and could be inhabited indefinitely, at a payable rent, by the people for whom they were intended.

Lily Altstad's apartment was on a tree-lined street wide enough to be a boulevard. But it was not a through street for traffic, and the sidewalks were wider than the pavement. Her front door was fourteen steps up from the portal. The stairs were of solid granite, and were only slightly worn. At the top were two identical doors side by side. Each opened into a corridor with a door and a stairway: the door to an apartment on the second story and the stairway to the apartments on the upper floors. It gave Altstad a good feeling to know that if his mother failed to pick up her mail from the pile that the postman wringed through the flap six mornings a week, the neighbors would knock on her door to make sure she was all right. She had weak lungs, and had recently returned from a stay in the sanatorium at Davos.

Lily kissed her son daintily on two cheeks and darted for the kitchen, where a kettle was whistling.

'Let me just put the *bolussen* in the oven and brew the tea.'

Whenever he came, she always had the same pastries from the Jewish bakery on the Churchill-laan: one ginger bun and one almond bun for each of them. They were baked like miniature loaves, and came in aluminum receptacles. You had to serve them hot to get the butter and oil in which they were drenched to ooze. They were the heaviest food Altstad knew, and if they were Turkish he knew he wouldn't touch them. But in his mother's house they were still a treat he could not resist.

'At five o'clock I have to go over to Jeanne. She lost her sister, poor thing. Eighty years old and still on her own, all her own shopping, in a walk-up apartment with two flights of steep stairs. She had a stroke and was gone in a week. That's the way I want to go, too, except I want to be able to talk to you in that week. In case I can't talk, you'll come and hold my hand, won't you? I'll know. And remember what I said. No surgery and no machines.

Let me go in peace. If you have to use a needle, use a needle. Anyway, they're sitting *shiva* at Jeanne's and a few of us are making a snack for the men when they come over for evening prayers.'

'I'm sorry about that, Moeder. Tell Jeanne I'm very sorry and send her my love.'

'I will. So tell me how are you.'

'Me? I'm fine.' Altstad could not start to tell his mother how he really felt. She only wanted to hear good news from him. For the first time in years, he resented this. No matter what happened, he would have to continue telling her that he was happy and prosperous. Even if his life came to an end, he could not take the logical steps to bring his body into line. By maintaining her sunny picture of him, she ruled over his life. He twitched at the thought that this sounded like Katy's complaint about him. Could he be that bad?

His mother read part of his mind.

'And how's your girlfriend in New York I never met?'

'She's doing great. She has a painting in an important exhibition next week.'

'That's nice. And?'

'And we still love each other.'

'Good. So?'

'So who knows? Maybe some day.'

'Maybe some day I'll have grandchildren? For great-grandchildren it's already too late, I hope you know.'

Leaving Lodewijk to mull over his debt to posterity and his mother, Lily went to the kitchen and came back with tea and *bolussen*.

'Mom, there's something I wanted to ask you about Katy. I love her a lot, and I thought I was showing it very nicely. It's hard on both of us that we can't be together all the time, but I've written to her every day since we started seeing each other.'

'That must be true love. To your own mother you never write.'

'I'm sorry. From now on I'll be better.'

'How long have you been saying that? If you only knew

how much pleasure it gives me to get a letter from you.'

'That's exactly it. The last time I saw Katy she said that my letters gave her too much pleasure. She said that they were too good to be true. She thought I used my imagination too much and I might be turning her into a dream. She even asked me not to write her any more letters for a while. Does that make sense to you?'

'I know exactly what she means. You're a dreamer. When you were little, you used to play make-believe all the time. More than other children. You remember that cute little girl Visser, what was her name? Grietje, Greetje? Anyway, I remember Mrs. Visser once talked to me when we were waiting in the schoolyard at lunchtime. She said she wasn't going to let Grietje? Greetje? come around to play with you any more, because you frightened her. You told her your real name was Mr. Six Million. You used to watch some stupid television program like that. You said you were from the year six million and she had to do everything you said. So maybe you frightened Katy too. You are lucky to have found such a smart girl. She is exactly what you need.'

'I said what?'

'I didn't hear you say anything.'

'No, what did I say to Greetje Visser?'

'That you were not from this world. You came from the future, and everyone had to do what you said. I told Mrs. Visser you were just making believe, but she didn't like the game. She had a point.'

'Did you talk to me about it?'

'I don't think so. I just kept an eye on you for a while when you played with little girls. You never did anything Mrs. Visser had to worry about.'

Altstad knew where to find Jan Mark Rigter at five o'clock on a Saturday afternoon: his psychoanalyst friend would be on a stool at his hangout, a living-room café behind the

Concertgebouw. The bar was not large, and was filled to over-flowing. The daily regulars occupied the chairs and tables, weekly regulars like Jan Mark took stools, and outsiders sat on the sofas or stood around uncomfortably, spilling over onto the street, although it was still too cold for that. Altstad was grateful for the crowd. When he walked in on the regulars, he always felt like an intruder. Now he wasn't noticed. There was also enough noise for him to be able to talk to Jan Mark without being overheard. Any good story told at this café found its way into print, often within half a day.

Jan Mark waved happily to Altstad, and ordered two glasses of *korenwijn* from the freezer.

'Lodewijk, are you just back from America again? Then please tell me an untranslatable joke. I haven't heard a good joke in weeks.'

'I wouldn't dream of it. Last time I told you a joke, you said I was acting out some filthy childhood frustration. It takes effort to forget all the nonsense you load on me.'

'This time I won't say a word, no matter how deliciously dirty the interpretation is. I'm dying for a good American joke.'

'All right. This man passes out on the street, and they call an ambulance for him. On the way to the hospital he comes to, and the paramedic asks him "Are you comfortable?" The man says "Thank God, I make a living."'

Jan Mark chuckled happily.

'Precious. Deep, too, but I won't tell you why.'

'I appreciate that.'

'Now what can *I* do for *you*? From the look on your face when you walked in, I knew that something is bothering you.'

'Here I thought I was fitting in so well. You're still pretty clever. Practicing psychoanalysis hasn't ruined you altogether.'

Jan Mark took a sip of his drink and looked at Altstad with affection and interest. A bubble of privacy formed around them.

'I had some scares in the past few days. I lose my focus on the surface of things and see past them. I go through the wallpaper.'

The mysterious Dutch expression was just right. Altstad tried to describe what happened in Central Park and at the Reynolds. He was too embarrassed to tell his friend what happened when he woke up and saw the girl in the Bronchorst. Maybe if it happens again, he thought.

'It's like someone inside me is seeing things behind everyday reality. I'm becoming a middleman in my own life.'

'Has anyone else noticed?'

'Yes, that's the other thing. For a few months I've been writing long letters to my girlfriend in New York. I write one every day I'm not with her, and that's more than half the time. Now she's asked me to stop because she thinks I am turning her into a figment of my imagination. When I told that to my mother this afternoon, she said that when I was a kid I had a runaway fantasy life and I used to say that I came from the future. I called myself the Man from Six Million.'

'What's going on in your work? Any unusual tension?'

'I guess you could say that. I have two very big deals on the fire. If both of them fall through, I'll be in bad trouble.'

Casually, Jan Mark took Altstad's wrist and looked at his watch.

'How's your health?'

'No complaints.'

'Are you getting enough sleep?'

'I haven't the least idea. When you cross the ocean twice in four days you kind of lose count.'

'Lodewijk, a psychiatrist is never at a loss for an explanation. I could give your condition a name and a prognosis. I could tell you how everything you are experiencing fits in: your work, your girlfriend, your childhood game, probably your father, your lack of sleep. But I won't do that unless you ask me to. It would fix things in a clinical picture, and make you into a case. I think you might have a better chance taking this thing on as a whole, functioning person. But let me tell you that what you are going through is no joke. It could change your life and personality. I wouldn't want to see that happen, because I like you too much the way you are.'

'What do you mean, take it on? What do you think is going to happen?'

'There's a good chance that things are going to get scary. Stay in touch with me. And get some sleep. If you walk me home I'll give you my free sample of the newest pills on the market.'

Since his divorce, Arnold Ungeleiter spent more time in shul. He was not used to being alone, and did not like it. It was not that he missed Rochelle, but he learned that he preferred her nudging to nothing at all. When they were together, he was able to watch television and ignore her. Now he could not keep his mind on a program. In the middle of the news, he would realize that he did not remember what the first item had been. He could concentrate better at the movies, but he always chose the wrong films. The last time he went he thought he was going to see a road-film comedy, but it turned out to be about homosexuals doing things he didn't want to know about, let alone see with his own eyes.

During the week it was not so bad. He stayed late at his office in the city, doing the paperwork that he used to neglect. At seven o'clock he would pick up the *Post*, eat at a dairy cafeteria on Sixth Avenue or a delicatessen on West 47th Street and then walk down to Times Square to catch the Seventh Avenue Express to Crown Heights. When he got home, he went through the mail. He filed his bank statements, comparing cancelled checks with stubs, put new bills into his reminder box and wrote checks for bills whose payment was due. He read the appeals from health campaigns, social causes and Jewish organizations. Anything Jewish or Israeli he would honor with donations of eighteen dollars. Drives against diseases that had killed members of his family would get ten dollars and charities for the homeless, the handicapped and the Third World got five, as long as none of the money was going to Christian churches or Arab countries.

The mail always contained offers for things he needed. Personally addressed letters described magazines he should be reading, clubs for discounted books and CDs, cheaper medical plans, brokerage and legal service than he now had, investment opportunities it would be foolish not to consider, lotteries which sounded like money in the bank, health clubs he should belong to. He felt obligated to read these letters, and if he agreed that the offer was sensible he would fill in the reply cards as long as they entailed no commitment. Mailings came in for cellular telephones, cooperative food-buying schemes, free credit on car purchases, funeral insurance, exterminators. Color folders contained special offers on products Rochelle used to buy, but which he would now have to explore himself: television sets and radios, air conditioners, refrigerators and freezers, alarm installations, carpeting. Sheets of newsprint were full of double coupons and double-double coupons for the local supermarkets, a system he did not understand but which he was sure would save him a lot of money if he would look into it. He found entire catalogues on his doormat of furniture, vacations, gift items and luxury goods. All of these things mattered to him, but he had no time to deal with them. How did other people do it? He felt as if life were slipping through his fingers.

The only personal letters he ever received were from his sister Beatrice in Los Angeles. She wrote about things which were not part of his life at all, especially her experiences as a volunteer in a hospice for terminal patients. He would just as soon not receive such letters, but he couldn't say that to his sister. Having received them, he would be happier not reading them, but he could not bring himself to do that. So he read miserably about people with cancer and Aids and how Beatrice tried to help them. The letters went on and on and never got anywhere.

Ungeleiter's divorce was a disaster. Rochelle had left him for his own partner, Ronald Giltman. They took a well-known society lawyer, while Ungeleiter was represented by his nephew Sidney. Sidney kept telling him gleefully how much money Rochelle and Giltman were throwing out by using such an expensive firm for a cut-and-dried case. When the judgment came down, Sidney was rooted to the spot. Ungeleiter had to take him by the arm out of the courtroom to the water cooler in the hall before he regained the power of speech. Not that he had anything to say. The award was larger than Ungeleiter's net worth. The next day, at her lawyer's office, Ungeleiter had to thank Rochelle for accepting their joint property and his share of the business as a final settlement. He was allowed to keep the lease on their rent-controlled apartment, where she hadn't lived since she moved in with Giltman. That afternoon she came to Crown Heights with the movers and emptied the place of everything except Ungeleiter's clothing, one bed, one table, one chair, one chest of drawers, Ungeleiter's desk, some cheap lamps and the books. She tagged the appliances and most of the furniture, linen and curtains for shipment to Ohio, where Giltman's daughter was starting dental school. At the last minute, she left the box with the dairy dishes and silverware behind. ('No way Sheila's gonna keep kosher,' she said.) She drove away in their car.

The next day Ungeleiter received a box with his personal effects, including some greasy girly magazines from the bottom drawer of his office desk, via UPS. By registered mail came a manila envelope from the lawyer containing: a letter in his own name, acknowledging receipt of all his possessions; his dismissal as director of Giltman & Ungeleiter; an announcement of the incorporation of the firm of Ronald & Rochelle; a notarized photocopy of the bill of sale of the name Giltman & Ungeleiter to Ronald & Rochelle for one dollar; a banker's check for fifty cents; a copy of an application by Ronald & Rochelle for a court order prohibiting Ungeleiter from using his name in business or from conducting business in hats and caps for a period of five years, under penalty of a fine of ten thousand dollars a day; a stamped jiffy bag addressed to the lawyer with a sticker on it asking him to send back all the keys he had to the premises of Giltman & Ungeleiter; and an invitation to the wedding of Ronald Giltman and Rochelle Ungeleiter née Schein at their country club. Ungeleiter put his signature at the crosses on the dotted lines, returned the papers and the rsvp card with regrets, and called Beatrice.

The only business Ungeleiter knew was jobbing hats and caps. When he started in the fifties, he bought from small manufacturers in lower Manhattan and sold to men's shops on Flatbush Avenue, Brownsville, East New York and the Rockaways. By the time he learned the routine, everything started to change. It was goodbye Humphrey Bogart, hello Jack Kennedy, and American men stopped wearing hats. Even Orthodox Jewish men started to walk to shul in small Israeli yarmulkes instead of homburgs and trilbies. Felt and wool gave way to cotton and synthetics, craftsmanship surrendered to mass manufacturing, small shops were edged out by discount chains, the margin from which Ungeleiter made his living was gutted by percentage players. His suppliers went out of business or moved south. The neighborhoods in Brooklyn and Queens disintegrated, and his retail customers closed one by one. Ungeleiter commiserated with the hatmakers, who retired and moved to Florida, and with the shop owners, who picked up franchises in Long Island shopping malls. He stayed behind, working for the few others like him who could not grasp the fact that the world they knew was gone forever.

He and Ronald Giltman became partners in 1963. Giltman had been a jobber, like Ungeleiter, but he had sold his business at the first offer, to a Taiwan group of cap manufacturers setting up their own sales network on the East Coast. They overpaid by so much that Giltman was able to buy a flagstone house in an exclusive new development in Westchester. The Chinese were unable to make Giltman's business work without him, and hired him as a consultant for more money that he had ever earned when he was on his own. From them he learned the import business. By the time he started a new firm, he knew how to get goods from Taiwan, Hong Kong and Korea into the country on the quota. He tapped the overcapacity of ambitious Asian manufacturers, buying run-ons of high-quality caps at prices lower than the brand-name labels were paying for products they had designed. Because he was always in Asia or Washington, he needed a partner at the office, and Arnold Ungeleiter was made to order: trustworthy, with a reputation for old-fashioned solidity and so unimaginative that he was above suspicion. Ungeleiter did the selling. With Giltman and Rochelle pushing him, he surpassed himself. Before long, he had salesmen on the road visiting independent mall shops from Washington to Boston. They charged higher prices than the chains, and paid a premium price to Giltman & Ungeleiter. Ungeleiter never found out that his Asian supplier, Tai-Man Caps, was a post-box firm wholly owned by Giltman, and that Tai-Man worked on a mark-up of one hundred percent.

By the time Rochelle left him, history was repeating itself. The mall shops were dying on the vine and the East Asians were being undercut by Southeast Asians and Latin Americans. Giltman decided that it was time to move downmarket, where he had no further use for Ungeleiter.

Out of the goodness of his heart, a phrase Ungeleiter heard once or twice a month from his brother-in-law, Mitchell Fleishig hired Ungeleiter to work at his old line of trade at a rented office on Broadway and 37th Street, for a firm financed by Fleishig. Rodeo East never got off the ground. Not only were the customers going out of business, but Tai-Man increased its prices by a good thirty percent. He could not understand how Ronald & Rochelle could sell the same items in their own discount outlets for less than he was paying the Taiwanese.

Before the divorce, Ungeleiter only went to shul on Friday evening and Saturday morning. With time hanging heavy on his hands over the weekend, he started appreciating that Jewish life had more to offer. He became a regular participant in services he had never thought of attending before. For morning prayers, he went to the right-lane-of-the-road Orthodox Jewish Center, as he always had. After lunch — usually at the house of friends, where the other guests invariably included a woman his age who had recently lost her husband or been divorced — and a nap, he would head for a study group at a Conservative synagogue in

Borough Hall. The Jewish Center also had a study group where they discussed the Bible reading of the week, but it was not for Ungeleiter. The young rabbi there delved into the holy commentaries printed in small, illegible letters in the margins of a traditional Bible edition paradoxically called The Big Letter Bible. He cultivated an accent you could cut with a circumcision knife and did not bother to translate Aramaic and Hebrew terms. Most of the time Ungeleiter had no idea what he was talking about. The rabbi in the Conservative shul spoke the King's English, and explained the Bible in modern terms. It was amazing how much wisdom the Bible contained about American politics, current events in Israel and race relations in Brooklyn. If Moses, the founder of the Jewish religion, had a black wife, how could anyone accuse the Jews of being racists?

For afternoon and evening services, Ungeleiter went to a chassidic shtibel, a house synagogue, in Crown Heights. Although all chassidim were ultra-Orthodox, these Hungarians were more moderate than the followers of the Polish and Lithuanian rabbis. They seemed more dignified to Ungeleiter, and they had more to eat. Afternoon prayers were always followed by a cup of tea and homemade sponge cake, and after the evening services and the leavetaking from the Sabbath Queen, everyone sat down for a light meal of herring and potato salad, with a glass of schnapps.

On this Saturday evening, returning from the shtibel, Ungeleiter found someone waiting for him at his doorstep. A man in a uniform of some kind asked him in an accent he could not place if he were Arnold Ungeleiter. When he said yes, the young man gave him a small envelope with something heavy in it.

'This is for you. You are kindly requested to remain near your telephone between two and three o'clock this morning.'

'Who are you? What is this?'

'That is all I can tell you.'

'I don't know you, you don't know me. Who gave you this?'

'You will certainly find out if you stay near your telephone. Goodbye.'

The man turned and walked away in a hurry. The envelope contained six keys taped together.

Although he thought he would be unable to fall asleep, Ungeleiter was in deep slumber, in front of the television set, when the phone rang. He fumbled with the receiver, not knowing why he was not in bed.

'Arnold, wake up. It's me, Mitchell.'

'Whaa?'

'Wake up, wake up. This is an emergency.'

'What's wrong? Is there anything the matter? Is it Beatrice?'

'There's nothing wrong, and Beatrice is fine. You have to do something for me. Are you with me now?'

'Yeah.'

'Did you get the keys?'

'The keys? Oh, yeah. Who was that man?'

'Never mind. You have to do something for me. Those keys will let you into the apartment of a friend of mine in Manhattan. He needs some stuff out here. He wants you to let yourself in and take those things and Federal Express them out to me. There may be more keys than you need, but that doesn't matter. The right ones have got to be there. Go get a pencil and paper.'

'Mitchell, what is this?'

'Stop asking me questions, Arnold, and just do what I say. We have no time for talk. I told you this is an emergency.'

'But you want me to go into the apartment of some stranger I don't even know. I can't do something like that.'

'You can't? I'll tell you something else you can't do. You can't collect your fucking salary this month.'

'Mitchell, why are you shouting at me? What's going on?'

'Okay, I'll try to keep calm. Let me repeat what I said. This is an emergency. This is something you have to do for me. You *have* to do it. So we are not going to talk about why it has to be done. You get that?'

'Well, if it's that important . . .'

'Yes, it's that important. So get a pencil and paper.'

Fleishig gave his brother-in-law Altstad's name and address and instructions on what to do in his apartment.

'And if anyone asks what you are doing there, you tell them you are doing a favor for Mr. Altstad. Got that? Not for me. Do not mention my name, no matter what.'

'What do you mean, no matter what? This is dangerous, isn't it?'

'Don't be a schmuck. It's not dangerous. Just behave normally, and what can happen? You let yourself into an apartment with the owner's key and you let yourself out again. Now get a move on. If that stuff isn't out here by Monday there's going to be real trouble.'

At 5 a.m., as Ungeleiter, his hands shaking, was trying the fifth key on the second lock in the door of Altstad's apartment, Penelope Hinsythe woke up. The creaks and slams of the house, day and night, were as familiar to her as the sloshing sounds of her own body. When she woke, she knew that she had been hearing unaccustomed noises for a while. Holding her breath and listening hard, she could tell that they were coming from an upstairs hallway. Without getting out of bed, she picked up the telephone and pushed autodial number 1.

'Saryl,' she whispered, 'there's someone in the house.'

Saryl Krieger looked at her clock and thought for a moment. 'Just one person?'

'I think so. I don't hear any voices. Do you want me to look?'

'No, stay in your apartment and keep quiet. Keep your ears open. Don't hang up. I'll be right here, and you tell me everything you hear. Now I have to put you on hold to make a call on the other line.'

Saryl's thriving gescheft, as Mr. Krieger called his wife's business enterprises, was not limited to real estate. She also owned a moving firm and a bagel service. From Saturday night to Sunday night two of the smaller trucks that during the week rode for Zalman Movers picked up batchloads from bagel factories in Queens and Brooklyn and delivered them to bakeshops all over the city. Both trucks had telephones. Mrs. Krieger dialed the one which was usually driven by a man who gave judo lessons in the Jewish Defense League.

'Yossel, where are you right now?'

'I'm crossing the 59th Street Bridge into Queens.'

'That's good. Listen, there's a burglar in my house on East 78th Street. I want you to go back across the bridge and head

straight for the house. Double-park a few doors away. I'm getting information from inside and I'll tell you what to do.'

'Just my cup of tea, Mrs. Krieger. I'm on the lower roadway,
so I can cut a U on the plaza. I'll be there in ten minutes.'

'Try to make it faster than that. Don't worry about the lights.'

'Lights? Never heard of them.'

'Where is your next pickup and your next delivery?'

'I was on my way to Reshefsky's in Astoria for a pickup. Mendy
was going to give me the delivery addresses.'

'I'll take over. My husband is already awake, I'll send him to
Reshefsky's in the station wagon. You put the bagels out of your
head until this business is taken care of.'

'Milady, your knight-errant is at your exclusive service.'

'Are you there, Penelope?'

'Yes, Saryl, I haven't been away. There is definitely someone in
the house. He must be in Mr. Altstad's apartment, since Mr.
Altstad is the only one who isn't home.'

'Good thinking. There's a lot of valuable art there. That must
be what he's after. Has he come down the stairs yet?'

'No. I heard him in the hall for a while, but now I don't hear
anything, so he must be in the apartment. He can't leave any
other way than the front door. You know the fire escape to the
roof is locked.'

'It's good you reminded me. In case we have to call the police,
be sure to unlock it before they arrive. But first we're going to try
to settle this without police. One of my boys is on his way. He'll
wait outside. I don't want anything to happen in the house. The
other tenants shouldn't know there was a burglar.'

Ungeleiter paused on the landing. Not a sound except for the
booming of his heart. He had done it. And he was glad. It was
exciting. Before opening the front door, he stopped again. Still
complete silence. He could not hear Penelope Hinsythe telling

Saryl Krieger 'He's leaving now' or Saryl Krieger saying to Yossel Berg 'Here he comes. Give him fifty feet.' When Ungeleiter had walked that far, he tripped over something he had not seen. He was saved from hitting his head on the pavement by a powerful hand that laid him down, twisted one arm behind his back and pinned his other beneath his body while a heavy knee nailed him face down to the sidewalk. The assailant felt his pockets, back, arms, underarms and legs.

'If you are armed, you'd better tell me now, otherwise you'll be very sorry.'

'Armed? What are you talking about, you meshuggenah? You attack me in the middle of the street and you ask me if *I'm* armed?'

A hand seized his jaw and turned his head around.

'Gottinhimmel, it's Mr. Ungeleiter!'

'Yossel!' Half a day earlier, the two men had shaken hands at the end of the Havdalah service at the shtibel and wished each other a good week, *A gute woch.*

'Yossel, what the hell are you doing to me?'

Berg picked Ungeleiter up and dusted him off.

'I'm sorry. If I knew it was you I wouldn't have tackled you. But you shouldn't have broken into Mrs. Krieger's house.'

'I didn't break in. Look, I have the keys. The tenant asked me to get something for him. A Dutch art dealer.'

'That's not what I heard.'

'Well, it's the truth. So you'd better let me go.'

'I'm sorry, but I've got to take you with me. We'll get this settled soon, you'll see. I'm sure it's a misunderstanding.'

'What do you mean, you've got to take me? Is this a citizen's arrest, or what?'

'No, I'm not taking you to the police station, I'm taking you to Mrs. Krieger.'

With his back against the inside front wall of the Portu-guese synagogue, Altstad shook his head in amazement at the audacity of Emanuel de Witte. He compared a Polaroid of de Witte's painting to what he saw. The picture space covered nearly the whole interior, a view which Altstad could take in only by moving his head through a wide arc. To produce a responsible depiction of the area covered in the painting, you would have to remove the front wall of the building and stand a block and a half away. De Witte had taken the laws of perspective into his own hands.

The camera Altstad had smuggled in had a zoom lens whose widest angle was at 35 mm. Waiting until he was alone in the building, he scanned the space and discovered that he needed twelve shots to get de Witte's composition onto film. Since the edges would be distorted, he would be better off with some extra overlap. He decided to break it down into twenty segments. There would be a lot of seams in his patchwork photo for Fleishig, but the view would be recognizable.

Before leaving the building he said the prayer for the dead. He did not go to synagogue except when forced by circum-stance, and when he did his first thought was always for his father. Not that his father had been exceptionally religious, but it was what a Jewish son did for his father. He lifted the hinged seat in one of the benches and took out a prayer book. With some difficulty, he located the Kaddish and mumbled it beneath his breath. He did not think it counted, since there was no service going on. But he supposed it was better than nothing. At least he could still read a little Hebrew, he thought. He remembered a story from a sermon he had heard at a bar mitzvah on Long Island. The rabbi said he had visited the

synagogue in Kiev and saw an old Jew reciting the Kaddish.
Out of sympathy, the rabbi asked for whom he was mourn-
ing. The man replied, 'My sons do not know Hebrew and do
not want to know they are Jewish. When I die, no one will
pray for me. So I am saying Kaddish for myself.' An urban
myth, no doubt, what they call in Dutch a monkey sandwich.
For the rabbi to tell it in the first person was a cheap homi-
letic trick. Still, it was effective. Every time the story crossed
Altstad's mind his eyes welled with tears.

As he left the synagogue, he heard a noise to his right. Near
the glass collecting bin on the Rapenburgerstraat, a bicycle had
fallen over. A man in a cap bent over to pick it up.

Altstad crossed the sordid Meester Visserplein, a planning
mistake of the kind for which Brezhnev put people up against
the wall. The lepers' hospital had stood here until it was demol-
ished in the mid-nineteenth century. In the nineteen-fifties they
dug a half-open traffic tunnel through it, under a big rounda-
bout for cars and trams. Pedestrians were provided with tunnels
of their own, which were eventually occupied by present-day
lepers. Junkies turned the tunnels into such unappetizing places
that they had to be sealed off, leaving big concrete stairwells
filled with garbage and leading into solid walls adorned with
graffiti.

It took three long traffic lights to get across the square. Altstad
walked half the length of the Maupoleum to the Uilenburgersteeg,
now a passage bridged by the upper stories of the building. He
turned onto the Houtkopersburgwal, where you could put garbage directly onto barges that took them out to the municipal
dump. At 11 o'clock Sunday morning, the station was closed
and no one was around. Altstad walked in the middle of the
street, toward the right bend into the Oude Schans. At the L-
shaped corner, he made an impulsive turn left, to have a quick
look at one of his favorite sights in Amsterdam. Whoever li-
censed the construction of the hideous Maupoleum had enough
of a conscience to protect the view of the Rembrandt House.
The monster office building stopped dead opposite the east wall

of the Rembrandt House. As misplaced as it may have been, this act of piety by barbarians always got to Altstad. It symbolized the guilt feelings toward culture that kept the Dutch art world alive in a mercantile, mercenary environment. It was the margin reserved grudgingly for his livelihood.

In the corner of his eye, Altstad noticed a bicyclist coming up from behind. Turning, he saw a man in a cap, not a Dutchman, steering a crooked path toward him. It was the man who had let his bicycle fall on the Rapenburgerstraat. He looked familiar, and Altstad stopped to try to place him. All at once, it came to him: it was the pale-skinned misfit from the sauna. A slow smile came over Altstad's face, and his hand started to go up in a greeting which could be turned into a brow-mop if the other failed to recognize him. As Altstad watched, the man clumsily passed something from his right hand to his left. It was a knife. Altstad pulled back in confusion, almost falling over a parking hazard one car width from the water. The bicycle was moving quickly, and the knife was a foot from his face when the rider went down. He rode straight into the hazard, and tumbled onto the quay. The knife clattered across the pavement and into the water. On his hands and knees, the man looked in desperation at Altstad. He crawled toward him, reaching out to grab a leg. Altstad jumped away, onto the corner of the quay. As the man gained his feet, a head popped up from a houseboat moored in the Oude Schans and called out, 'What the hell is going on?' The attacker looked around him unhappily, at the bike, the water, the houseboat dweller and Altstad, then broke and ran back, limping, in the direction from which he had come. He disappeared under the Maupoleum. The other two watched him go.

'What was that all about?'

'I have no idea. The guy was bearing down on me with a knife when he hit the pole. Did you ever see him before?'

'No. Anyway, will you please remove the bike.'

'Me? Oh, yeah, yeah, all right.'

He crossed the street with the bike. The front wheel was bent.

It was a beat-up old granny bike, full of stickers. Obviously stolen, no point in trying to trace it. He carried it down the Houtkopersburgwal to a bicycle rental place near the corner. They would bring it back into circulation or throw it on the barge.

While the attack was going on, Altstad had not felt a thing except a rush of indignation. Now, walking for the second time toward the Oude Schans, he began to realize what almost happened to him. If he had not gone off to the left, the man on the bike would have come up on him from behind and stabbed him in the back. Right now he would be lying on the pavement with a punctured lung, bleeding and choking to death. He walked past the apparition, feeling sick and scared. Within three minutes he was home. He locked the door and sat down on a kitchen chair, trembling and nauseous.

When the telephone rang, he did not move. Not until he heard the voice of the caller leaving a message did he even turn toward the phone.

'This is Mrs. Krieger. I am sorry to be calling you at this early hour, but someone has been inside your apartment and we caught him. We don't want to let him go before we talk to you. So if you will call me back as soon as you can. We cannot keep him here forever, of course . . .'

'Hello, Mrs. Krieger, it's me. I'm not feeling very well, and I wasn't going to answer any calls. But when I heard what you said, I thought I'd better pick up.'

'Is that you in person, Mr. Altstad? Yes? Do you know someone named Arnold Ungeleiter? He's the man who was in your apartment.'

'No, I never heard the name. Who is he?'

'He's Jewish, he's middle-aged, he's from this neighborhood, Crown Heights, and he's in the hat and cap business. He has nothing to do with Europe or with art. So we didn't believe him when he said that he went into the apartment to do you a favor. I couldn't imagine how he could know you, and he wasn't able to explain. But he did have keys to all the doors, including the front door. You didn't make copies of the keys, did you? You know the rules.'

Her voice narrowed in timbre and modulated a major second up the scale. Altstad heard the chain saw coming on. He hoped his answer did not sound overanxious.

'No, Mrs. Krieger, I would never do that. I know better than to do that.'

'He *had* the keys. But they were funny copies. Maybe European. Instead of half-circles on both sides, they are like six-sided. Have you ever seen a set like that?'

'You're right, it does sound as if they were made in Europe. Someone must have copied my keys here. What did he take?'

Altstad asked it less out of concern for his goods than to change the subject.

'That's the funny part. I was sure he was after your art. You have all that valuable old art. But he didn't take any of that. All he took were some sheets of stationery and a tape cassette.'

'Stationery?'

'Yes, it says 'Lodewijk Altstad Fine Art' with your addresses and telephone numbers and bank account numbers and your chamber of commerce number.'

'Why would anyone want that?'

'We thought maybe you would have an idea. Do you want to know what's on the tape?'

'Yes, please.'

'It must come from your answering machine. There are a lot of messages on it. Most of them are from the same person. Mitchell. He gets madder and madder, telling you to call him back or he'll murder you.'

Ineke van der Heyden drove Altstad to Schiphol in time for the KL 601 to Los Angeles, the same flight Fleishig had taken twenty-four hours earlier. On the way, he gave her the roll of black-and-white film he had shot in the Portuguese synagogue that morning.

'When you have the montage, fax it to Fleishig at this number. Don't forget to remind me at the airport to scribble a covering note. If he calls, say that I just left your studio and that I'm taking a train for Groningen to stay overnight with friends. Say that he can reach me at home tomorrow evening.'

'Why are you doing this, Lodewijk?'

'Weird things are going on. Not only that business on the Oude Schans I told you about. I also got a call from my landlady in New York that someone got into my apartment in New York last night. Both incidents are connected to Fleishig. And he's got my painting. I have to get it back, and that will be easier if he doesn't know that I'm coming to Los Angeles.'

'I thought there was something wrong with that man when he was in my studio.'

Altstad suppressed a surge of annoyance. Why did such gems of intuition always come out *after* they pan out? What annoyed him even more is that Ineke was right. Fleishig did behave strangely on his visit, and Altstad had pretended to himself not to notice it.

'Why don't you call the police?'

'What could I tell them? That a man fell off a bike with a knife in his hand and then ran away? That someone let himself into my New York apartment with a spare set of keys and took some sheets of paper and a cassette tape worth about ninety-nine cents?'

He heard the sarcasm in his own voice and managed to shut up for a minute. He hoped that he had not succeeded in making Ineke feel foolish, which is what he half intended.

'First I would have to convince the Amsterdam police and the New York police that I was being victimized, and then get them to convince the Los Angeles police that Fleishig was behind it. I'm not even sure of it myself. Anyway, that would take days or weeks, and Fleishig might sell the painting tomorrow. The paper the burglar took in New York is the kind I write invoices on. I think Fleishig is going to forge an invoice for the de Witte for a low price, sell it for a lot and pocket the difference himself.'

'But he can't do that now that the burglar got caught, can he?'

'I'm letting the burglar send it to Fleishig as if nothing went wrong. I don't want him to know that I'm on to him.'

'Won't the burglar call Fleishig and tell him what happened?'

'He's been sent off to an all-day prayer session at a Jewish camp in New Jersey. They're going to make sure he doesn't get to a phone.'

'You kidnapped him?'

'Just for a day. He'll enjoy himself.'

'What about the man who tried to kill you?'

'Even if he gets in touch with Fleishig and admits that he screwed up this morning, Fleishig will have no reason to think I suspect him.'

'If you're right, what you're doing is very dangerous. Should you be going in on your own?'

'I have a friend in Los Angeles who will help me. He's picking me up at the airport. And what you're doing is terrific. You're covering my rear.'

'You keep your rear in one piece, Lodewijk, and I'll cover it.'

Altstad politely declined the headphones. With an eleven-hour flight ahead of him, he knew he should sleep. But he almost never got a good rest on a plane. He could not risk swallowing one of Rigter's freebees. When he landed he had to be off to a running start.

He accepted a refill of champagne and tried to read the *Sunday Times* but could not get much deeper than the headlines. After lunch and a cognac, he settled into a story on the London art market. The demand for Old Masters was still shrinking. There was a round-up of the usual explanations. Fly-by-night mentality of the eighties responsible for excessively high prices. Needful corrective. True quality will always retain its value. Blablabla.

Altstad got up to stretch his legs. When he returned to his seat, he glanced out of the window at the sea 30,000 feet below. He was astounded to see that the plane was heading down. He felt the upward pull of a dive, and his stomach began to turn. He strapped himself in, grabbed the seat handles and waited for the pilot to explain what was happening. No explanation came. The pilot must have passed out, he thought. So that's how I die.

The sensation of dropping became stronger. Altstad was sure he would have hit the ceiling of the plane if it weren't for the safety belt. His eyes were half-closed and unseeing. Although he thought he might throw up, he could not bring himself to reach for a bag. He was too petrified to move.

'Would you like another drink, sir?'

The flight attendant was trying to fool him into thinking nothing was wrong. They must be trained to do that, he thought. He turned toward her slowly. She was smiling at him from across the vacant seat between them. How did she stay on her feet? He nodded from side to side, slightly so as not to aggravate his nausea. When he faced front again, he caught sight once more of the sea rushing up toward him. He pulled the blind down and sat back rigidly for a ten-hour plunge to Los Angeles.

'Are you Mitchell Fleishig?'

Oh boy, thought Fleishig, this is it. Oh boy, Oh boy. He knew the voice from the telephone last Tuesday morning. Only now he was not hearing it through the telephone. It came from the unseen head of a man standing over him with a gun, next to the open door of his car. He had driven into his garage, and the man had opened the car door and was pointing a gun at him.

'Yes.'

'Put your hands as far front as you can reach.'

Fleishig did, and the man patted him down slowly and thoroughly.

'Give me the keys and stay where you are.'

The man closed the driver's door and walked around the front of the car to the passenger's side, keeping the gun pointed at Fleishig. Fleishig did not think he ever saw him before, and he couldn't account for his instantaneous impression that the man looked like a golf pro. Sporty but not athletic, with a forgettable square-jawed face, a striped seersucker jacket, sunglasses and a cloth hat. He got into the passenger's seat and looked through the glove compartment. He released Fleishig's seat belt and fastened his own. Then he handed the keys back.

'Open the garage door with the remote, back out slowly, come to a stop and close it again.'

Fleishig did as he was told.

'Get onto the Santa Monica Freeway going west.'

This sounded very bad. Fleishig was thinking fast, but he wasn't getting any ideas. Beatrice wasn't home and no one knew where he was. His mind raced in neutral. Although he was afraid of what he might hear from his passenger, he could not keep himself from talking to him.

'Are you the person who called me the other day?'

'Yes.'

'I remember our conversation very well. You told me I had until Tuesday morning to come up with the one point eight two.'

'So?'

'So it's Sunday.'

'Right.'

'So like what's going on?'

'You'll see.'

Worse answers were imaginable, but Fleishig could not pretend to be reassured. He wondered if there was anything he could do. In the movies, people regularly escaped from situations like these. They spun their cars around and their passengers flew out of the door; they braked suddenly and knocked their captors out or hit them in the Adam's apple; they maneuvered themselves into surgical collisions; they jammed their horns to get the attention of the police. Fleishig could excuse himself for not attempting any such heroics. Even if by some out-of-the-way chance he succeeded, that would hardly induce Benny Santangelo to back off and forget about the whole thing. He drove fifty-five, as carefully as he could. He was in Beatrice's old Mitsubishi, which shimmied at fifty and pulled right at sixty. He had turned in the Mercedes 580 to the lease company the day after his talk with the bank.

Past Fourth Street, the freeway went into a short tunnel. Beyond it, the road dipped to reveal the vastness of the Pacific Ocean. As long as Fleishig lived in Los Angeles, he had never gotten used to the sight. It was imposing, but there was something not right about it. For one thing, it was on the wrong side. The ocean should be east of the continent, not west. And it was too empty. In New York, there was a harbor full of islands and ships and action. The Statue of Liberty always brought a lump to his throat. It reminded him of Europe and the sufferings of his grandparents before they came to the New World. He even got a warm feeling about the Irish and Italians and Poles who came with them and made it in America in their own way. There was so much history in the Atlantic, so much dignity. The Pacific was empty. All it made you think about was surfing, yachting, beach parties, coke, sex with girls you just met. Catalina Island instead of Ellis Island, lots of water and then Pearl Harbor, Hiroshima, Vietnam, Sonyland. California was all a big mistake. If he got out of this, Fleishig thought, he would move back to New York. Who would still remember why he left?

'Stay on P.C.H.'

Pacific Coast Highway ran below an unproud earthen cliff that crumbled into the sea as you watched. Geology with a human face. How about a nice miracle, thought Fleishig. An earthquake to bring down the palisade. They would think he was dead, and he would escape to Wyoming and live in a survivalist camp. As long as the gunman didn't tell him to turn right into a canyon. That would mean pulling off the road into an empty spot in the hills and getting shot. If the man told him to turn right he would crash the car. Run back to the house, sell the painting and bring the money to Benny Santangelo. Declare bankruptcy and go back home with Beatrice to New York. The man said nothing. They passed the turn-offs to Topanga Canyon and Cold Canyon. As they neared the stoplight at Malibu Canyon Road, he spoke.

'Get in the left lane and take a U at the light.'

The car began to tremble as Fleishig slowed down, and he shook with it. He might survive the afternoon after all. They were going to drive to a house on the beach at Malibu. This must be where Benny Santangelo lived. If he wanted Fleishig killed, he wouldn't do it in his own home, would he? About half a mile south, they pulled into the driveway of a yellow frame house.

'Honk the horn once.' The man never said a word too much, thought Fleishig. He could learn from that. He himself was always shooting off at the mouth, especially when he was nervous. This afternoon he would try to say less.

A minute later, the garage door opened, and Fleishig was instructed to drive in. His door was opened by another golf pro. He got out of the car and was led into the house. Benny Santangelo was on a patio overlooking the beach, fixing a barbecue.

'Hiya, Mitchell, glad you could join us. Honey, this is Mitchell Fleishig. I told you about him, remember, the real estate developer with the art collection. My wife is into art too, Mitchell, she does Japanese flower arrangements. It's not like the chichi Dutch painters you collect who are so special that no one even heard of them, but it's very creative anyway.'

'Pleased to meet you, Mrs. Santangelo,' Fleishig said to the strawberry blonde on the couch.

'That's my sister-in-law, sir. She's also a honey, if you get to know her. But I don't think she's for you. My wife is in the kitchen.'

There were chuckles all around as Fleishig looked for the kitchen. He found it at the far end of the patio, where another strawberry blonde was up to her elbows in a big glass bowl filled with sausages, chops and ribs in blood-colored marinade.

'Pleased to meet you, Mrs. Santangelo.'

More chuckles. It occurred to Fleishig that he was not applying his new lesson about the spare use of language all that well.

'The house drink is guava daiquiris with homemade Sicilian mandrake liqueur. You tell me what you think of it.'

Santangelo wiped his hands on his apron and walked to the bar. He put ice cubes into the mixer, poured a lot of rum over them, squeezed a lime, strained some sugar and spooned guava flesh into the mixture and then blended it all for a minute. With exaggerated care he poured the mixture into an ice-cream soda glass.

'Now for the secret ingredient.'

Taking a plain brown bottle off the top shelf, Santangelo poured a few drops of the contents along a glass rod into the drink.

'You don't want to bruise the little fella.'

He stirred gently, put an orange blossom on top, inserted a silver straw and extended the drink ceremoniously with his left hand to Fleishig while shaking right hands with him.

'We cross arms as a holy pledge to honor each other. You are my guest, Mitchell, and that creates a bond. Do you accept my hospitality?'

'By all means, Mr. Santangelo.'

'Why are you so formal all of a sudden? Call me Benny.'

Santangelo picked up his own drink and clinked glasses with Fleishig.

'Let us drink to the sanctity of our bond.'

'Yes, let us.'

Fleishig felt lame and silly. If they were going to shoot him or poison him, why didn't they get it over with? Why were they toying with him? He took a long sip. He was too shaken to pay attention to the taste.

'How do you like it?'

'It's a very exceptional drink. I have never tasted anything like it.'

'It does things for you. You'll see.'

The main floor of the house was one big room opening onto the patio. Fleishig walked around the room uncomfortably. His eye was caught by a painting over the flagstone fireplace. A reclining nude smiled sweetly at the beholder. Her inviting form was laid in broadly with a palette knife in pink and beige and strawberry blonde.

'Nice painting, huh? That's the kind of art everybody appreciates. A beautiful woman showing her beauty. The artist wasn't trying to impress anyone, just please them. That's the sort of thing you should collect. Take it from me.'

Untying his apron, Benny Santangelo gestured to Fleishig.

'While the charcoal is getting a glow on, you and I are going to take a stroll on the beach.'

A wooden staircase descended from the patio, over a flagstone terrace, to an enclosure with a swimming pool and a putting green. At the far end was a beach house over the full width of the plot. It was decorated like a stylized triumphal arch, with a big double barn door in the center. Inside was a complete gym, a pool table and a ping-pong table.

'Below us is the bunker. We have a shelter down there that the whole family can live in for as long as we have to. Do you know how long that is? Do you know what the half-life is of strontium 90? Most people don't. They spend a lot of money on shelters that they are going to have to leave before the outside world is safe. When they start running low on water and supplies, who is going to leave first? I'm not going to subject my family to those horrors. Our shelter is equipped for bearable living for six people for twenty-five years. Complete with entertainment and work-out equipment and a chapel. It's famous on the beach, or should I say infamous. There were a lot of complaints. The excavation and construction and stocking took four years. Although many people know about it, I assure you that none of them know where the entrance is. It cannot be found. We sometimes have special guests down there, but they don't find out where the entrance is either.'

Behind the beach house was a boat shed with kayaks and surf planks.

'I have a nice sixty-foot yacht at the marina. You have to come with us on a cruise to Baja sometime. But first we have to get our business straightened out. Do you have anything you want to tell me?'

'Just one thing, sir, Benny. And that is that on Tuesday you will have your money.'

'I'm glad to hear that. If you say so, it must be true, and I have to believe you. But I must say that this conflicts with my information. I made some inquiries about you this week. I should have done that at the start, of course, but you know how it is. Sometimes you're so busy or so trusting that you skip steps. That's always a bad idea, and I must say that this experience with you has taught me a lesson. From now on, no more art as security. I had no idea how unliquid art is. So tell me, where is the money coming from that you're going to pay me back on Tuesday? This interests me a great deal, since it turns out you are worth less than nothing.'

Fleishig began trembling again. Slogging through the sand, he was getting short of breath. He should take better care of his body, he thought. Santangelo was a good thirty pounds lighter than him, and the effort had no visible effect on him. His answer came out in gasps.

'You may be skeptical about this, in the light of what you just said. Because as it happens, in point of fact, the money is still in the form of a painting. But I assure you that this painting is liquid. I may have to sell it somewhat below its worth to turn it into cash in a day, but the kind of painting this is, it is instantly saleable.'

'I see. Well, how come this wonder painting is not part of the security for your loan?'

'Because I just bought it.'

'When?'

'Over the weekend.'

'In Palm Springs, right?'

'Yes.'

They had reached the hard sand at the edge of the water. The surf was feeble, and there was little wind. It was quiet, and it got quieter with every second of Santangelo's silence. Fleishig stared at the horizon, wondering whether this was his last sunset.

'Mitchell, you are a guest in my house, you meet my family, you seal a bond with me, and what do you do? How do you repay my hospitality? You dump on me the biggest load of horseshit anyone has ever tried to load off on me.'

Fleishig sighed into the sun. It was true, what could he say?

'I will try not to get upset, because it isn't worth it. You are not worth it, someone who would not only abuse my trust on a loan but lie to me in my own house. I know a lot of people in Palm Springs, and on the average I would say they are richer and smarter than most of the other people I know. But even if they were the stupidest people on earth, there would be no one in Palm Springs stupid enough to sell you on Saturday a painting on which you could clear on Monday almost two million dollars. And you think that I am even stupider than that, because you expect me to swallow this giant load of horseshit.'

By the time he finished speaking, Santangelo was shouting at the top of his lungs, and Fleishig was shaking uncontrollably.

'Do you know who is going to swallow shit, Mitchell? You are. You and your wife.'

Fleishig's knees buckled and he fell onto the sand. He was crying in loud sobs.

Santangelo took a deep breath and lowered his voice.

'It is a very good thing you have no children, because I would not like any child to see happen to their parents what is going to happen to you and your wife.'

'My wife didn't do anything.'

'That is the tragedy of it. All she did wrong was marry you, a slimeball kike who gives his people a bad name and tries to jerk off the wrong guy.'

Fleishig was blubbering. 'I swear you'll have the money. Don't do anything to my wife.'

'Get on your feet, you turd. The neighbors can see you.'

They started back for the house.

'Where is the painting now?'

'At my place.'

'Are you expecting anyone to be there?'

'No.'

'Your wife?'

'She won't be home until nine or ten.'

'Okay. Here is what we are going to do. You give your house keys and alarm code to George, you tell him where the painting is, and he brings it here. In the meanwhile, I get my art dealer over and we all look at the painting together and you tell me where and how you got it.'

In the boat house, Santangelo stamped on the ground.

'We are standing on top of a dome of reinforced concrete lined with lead. It was finished the week the wall came down in

Berlin. On the beach they laughed at me. Santangelo's Folly. Very original. We'll see who laughs last.'

The charcoal briquets were at their hottest, starting to turn to gray ash. Tongues of flame lapped at the meat that Santangelo laid down on the grill.

'I hope you enjoy the barbecue, Mitchell. I go to great pains to get the best cuts.'

'. . . immediate loading and unloading of passengers only.'

Altstad left the air-conditioning of Tom Bradley International Terminal for the warm, dirty airbath of outdoor Los Angeles. He let Sy Triolo help him into the front seat of his car, parked at the curb.

'The white zone is for immediate loading . . .' The door slammed on the famous mechanical voice and a bass clarinet played a scale up, down and around 'The Way You Look To-night' before his friend got behind the wheel and took off. The floor of the Chevrolet station wagon was littered with beer bottles and parking tickets. Altstad leaned back and smiled.

'There's a Hockney opening on Main, an all-star gospel concert at the Hollywood Bowl, a pre-season night game at Dodger Stadium, Phil Woods is playing at a lounge in Brentwood, Junior Wells is at the Western and the line on Arizona for all the sushi you can eat was only half a block long an hour ago. You pick it, tatele. I am all yours, because it is so great to see you. How come you look so terrible?'

'I had an awful flight, don't ask me why. I thought I was going to die. Seeing you picked me up a lot. As soon as I spotted you, I thought at least there was one person in the airport who looked worse than me.'

'Don't be fooled by appearances. My condition is stable. I am pickled in smog and have looked exactly this way for years. You, on the other hand, were rather dashing last time I saw you. How come you have no baggage? You look like a refugee. Last night on television there were Albanians trying to get into Italy. That's what you look like. Like you have been living under a Maoist tyranny all your life and have never been allowed to press your clothes and have been eating nothing but canned cabbage soup since you were weaned. But don't worry about a thing anymore, baby, because I am going to take care of you. We're going to start off with scungilli and slammers on the pier to bring you back to life and then we are going to snort a line and then pick up some girls and get them to manicure us before we ball them. And then, and then we'll figure out what to do with the evening. Luigi, how ya been?'

'Not bad, in some ways very good. I'll tell you all about it soon. But first I need your help. The reason I have no baggage is that I had to catch a plane in a big hurry. I found out that someone from Los Angeles, a customer of mine, is trying to kill me, and he's stolen a valuable painting that belongs to my aunt. I have to get the painting back right away, right now.'

'This kind of thing happens every day, you wouldn't believe it. O tempora, o mores. But that's no reason to sit back and let them kill your friends, I always say. Just tell me where this fucker lives and on the way fill me in on the details.'

'Cañon between Carmelita and Elevado.'

'Pooh, pooh. We are on our way. Your painting is as good as retrieved. It is already in the back of this very car.'

Half an hour later, they were parked across the street from Fleishig's darkened house on Cañon, a hundred feet up the road. Triolo walked up and down the block.

'Silent as the ever-loving grave. My considered judgment is that there is no one in that house, not a soul. We can do one of two things. We can break and enter or we can wait for someone else to open the door and turn the lights on so we can see what is going on. If you want my professional opinion, I say wait. The Venice police have grown accustomed and inured to the spectacle of me setting off my own alarm, as I do once or twice a month when I come home so happy that I forget what kind of society we live in. But I have not had the opportunity to condition the Beverly Hills police to yawn when I set off someone *else's* alarm. You should have given me a few days. Although I have the strong suspicion that the Beverly Hills police are more shall we say property-sensitive than the Venice police. And you do realize that we are practically in punting range of their very headquarters.'

Altstad did not have to answer. As Triolo was winding down his speech, an old Mitsubishi passed them, slowed down, signalled a left turn and pulled into Fleishig's driveway.

'Did you see the driver? Is that the guy?'

'I don't think so, but I'm not sure.'

No one got out of the car. The garage door opened automatically and the car disappeared inside. They waited.

'Isn't this interesting? There are still no lights going on. Here we were waiting for someone to make the place a little homelike, maybe put on some music and set a pot of coffee, and what do we get? A lover of darkness. If I had a suspicious nature, which thank the Lord on bended knee I do not, I would say there was a prowler in that house. A prowler with a key and a code. What do you make of that, ladies and gentlemen? What is the night visitor after? Should we ring the bell and ask? No, say I, we wait and see.'

After a long ten minutes, the garage door opened again and the car pulled out. The same driver still seemed to be alone in the car.

'What goes up must come down, Lolo. Walk back to the corner of Carmelita and play bystander. When the action starts, you mime morbid curiosity and ascertain whether your painting is or is not on the mobile premises. If it is, you let me know and I do something to the man behind the wheel to make sure he does not get in the way while you load the painting into my car. Go.'

As Altstad walked toward the corner, Triolo made a U-turn and began driving in the same direction in front of the Mitsubishi. He stopped at the corner. It was a four-way intersection with no traffic lights. There were stop signs for traffic coming from all directions. First come, first cross. When the Mitsubishi was twenty feet behind him and slowing to a halt he threw the Chevrolet into reverse. Accelerating as fast as he could, he rammed the knob of his trailer hook through the radiator of the Japanese car. A cloud of steam went up and boiling green water flooded the street.

Altstad hadn't reached the corner yet. He left the sidewalk and approached the crash as casually as he could. The driver of the Mitsubishi was not impressed by his performance. He stepped out of the car and reached into his jacket for a pistol. He turned right to fire a shot through the steam in the direction of Triolo and then swung his arm back left, pointing the gun at Altstad's stomach. Altstad had broken into a forward run. Now he turned his shoulder to the man and leaped at him as the gun went off. He collided into the gunman, unaware whether all of the impact he felt was the collision or whether he had been hit.

The driver had the wind knocked out of him. He doubled over in pain, retching. Altstad kicked the gun out of his hand toward the curb, looked into the car and saw nothing. He bent over the driver for the keys and opened the trunk. There was the travelling case he had given Fleishig. He took it out, ran around the Mitsubishi and shoved it through the open back window of Sy Triolo's station wagon. Triolo was standing beside the open door of his car holding his shoulder, covered with blood and glassy-eyed. Altstad eased him into the back seat of the car, got behind the wheel and drove away. There were cars at every corner of the intersection. No one got out and no one followed the Chevrolet as it drove down Cañon and joined the stream of traffic on Santa Monica Boulevard. Altstad was breathing hard and hurting from the flying crash, but he was not wounded.

'Well done, Lodewijk. I never knew that you pretty little Dutch boys were such potent dudes.'

'Where are you hit, Sy?'

'In the shoulder, buddy, with a million-dollar wound. This is the wound I have been dreaming about since Khe Sanh. Literally, I'm sorry to say. A few times a month, alternated with dreams about different kinds of wounds I like you too much to tell you about. Thanks to you, I can now call this golden wound my own. You fly in from Amsterdam and in an hour you save my life and free me from fear. So tell me, who else in Los Angeles is trying to kill you? One more hit like this may cure me of my bashfulness.'

'Hey, be serious, which hospital should I take you to?'

'A hospital is definitely not the ticket. In hospitals they know not from discretion, and that is our first need tonight. Stories about gunshot wounds they share with the police. And when I passed the bar in California, they made it clear to me that the police were supposed to answer my questions and not the other way around. There was a list of no-nos, and I seem to recall that it covered such items as vehicular assault, willful destruction of property, abetting attempted manslaughter, fleeing the scene of an accident and receiving stolen goods.'

'Restolen goods.'

'Maybe in Europe you can afford to make nice distinctions like that. You people are so civilized. I love you for it, though many others don't. If we were that refined, we would have to give this land back to the Indians. I mean, if we were half that refined, we would not have stolen the country from the Indians in the first place. So, no hospital please. Now that we are on the subject, though, I do have an idea. Take the Harbor Freeway to Manchester and I will guide you to the home of an old medic I know from Can Tho. This man has a discretion-guaranteed infirmary in his garage where more gunshot wounds get treated on a Saturday night than on M.A.S.H. in a whole month. Sunday is a quiet day, the Lord's Day in the barrios, so we won't have to wait in line too long. And then we pick up where we left off. You've had enough time to think about it, so stop stalling, bubba. What's it gonna be, gospel or blues?'

'In the Name of Allah, the Compassionate, the Merciful. The Inevitable: and what is the Inevitable? Would that you knew.'

On a bench between two trees in a row of cypresses, Altstad sipped a cool drink, pondering the depths of the verse while losing himself in the intricacy of the tiled inscription. Did the calligraphy itself, which tied the words into an inextricable knot, signify inevitability? He listened for a clue in the loud hiss and splash of the forty-eight jets of water arcing into the long pond. As the breeze shifted, the perfume in the air modulated from false orange to jacaranda, interspersed by a stab of jasmine.

He walked slowly down the arcade, with its potted citrus trees and trimmed hedges of boxwood. In the niche at the far end he found the Koran's explication of its own question: 'We have made all things according to a fixed decree. We command but once: Our will is done in the twinkling of an eye.' Could the course of life really be inevitable, dictated by an ordained code? How can we know? How can creatures living in time know if they were determined by something outside of time?

From the opposite end of the arcade a figure approached, smiling and gesticulating in friendly welcome. He was tall and what the Koran would call comely, dressed and groomed in understated good taste.

'Lodewijk, what an unexpected pleasure. I'm sorry to have kept you waiting.' His voice was mellifluous and sincere. He was a former teacher of Altstad's at the Institute and was now director of the Mitty Museum in Pasadena, a reconstruction of the Generalife in Granada twenty-five percent larger than life.

'I'm glad you were able to squeeze me in at such short notice, Jackson.'

'So am I. You know how delighted I always am to see you. Would you like another julep?'

'Not right now. It sounds ungracious, after you agreed to see me unannounced, but I'm in a hurry to show you the painting I've brought. There is a special reason for haste that I'll explain after you see it.'

Jackson Hampshire opened a door in the long back wall of the arcade. Altstad knew where they were going, but he still had to swallow hard as he crossed the threshold. From the dazing light of thirteenth-century Spain, they crossed in one step into the candlelight glitter of the *ancien régime*, given extended life in the style rooms of the Mitty. The lamented founder of the museum had felt a special kinship not only to the caliphs of Moorish Spain but also to the kings of France. Although he was worth more when he died than Louis XIV had ever been, he sensed rightly that this was not going to cut any ice with posterity once the estate had been settled. So he left everything to the museum, as his best crack in the long run at keeping the company of his proper peers.

They walked past the sun king in all his glory, gazing eternally across the gallery at a painting of a half-naked girl with an unbearably delectable bottom doing things with a little dog that made you wish you were a little dog. Nearby was Hampshire's office, where they took the de Witte out of its case and put it on a study easel.

Altstad did not have to explain to Hampshire what he was seeing. Hampshire was one of the few people who knew the de Witte at first hand. Altstad had brought him to Aunt Juliana for tea eight years before, when Hampshire was in Amsterdam for the opening of an exhibition. He would not have forgotten the painting or confused it with any of the other versions. He looked hard at it for a few minutes, not saying anything.

'Interested?'

'You know I am. What made your aunt decide to sell?'

'To help me out.'

'The best reason. How does this hold up to the version in the Rijksmuseum?'

'To my mind the composition is more interesting. And as far as I can tell, the condition of this painting is better. In any case, I am sure there will be no unpleasant surprises when you strip it.'

Altstad was proud but also ashamed to realize that he had applied one of Molenaar's selling injunctions to a good friend: as soon as the customer shows serious interest, shift to the advisory mode, as if the painting is already theirs.

'What's the price?'

'Two and a half. I know I could hold out for more, but I need a quick yes.'

'That may be too high for a quick decision. How hard is that figure?'

'It's discussable.'

'All right, what's the mystery?'

'Do you know a Los Angeles collector named Mitchell Fleishig?'

'Do I? Whenever I introduce a speaker in our lecture series, Fleishig is up in the front row looking bright-eyed and bushy-tailed, with a notebook and a pen. He's the only one in the audience who takes notes, and he sits where he can pick up reflected light from the screen. He monopolizes the speakers after the lecture, lavishing them with praise and inviting them and me to lunch or dinner and a look at his collection. I've been along twice, and it actually is not a bad bunch of paintings. The Utrecht masters he buys from you are adding up nicely. For general coverage of the Dutch school it doesn't begin to compare to the Hadley collection, of course, but for Utrecht it's better. You don't expect something as subtle as that from . . .'

'From such a gross character. I know you're too polite to finish the sentence, Jackson.'

'As long as you don't tell anyone else I said it. Well, what does Fleishig have to do with the de Witte? I would have thought it was out of his range.'

'Me, too. But he flew over to Amsterdam last week in a Blitzkrieg operation and took the painting back with him. He said he had to show it to a group of people who wanted to make a donation of a major painting in the name of a Jewish cause. Have you heard anything about this?'

'No. But that doesn't say anything.'

'If you had it would make a difference. Anyway, the day after Fleishig left, strange things started happening to me. In Amsterdam, a man who Fleishig showed me to in a sauna tried to kill me on the street.'

'What?'

'I know it sounds absurd, but there it is. On Friday evening, Fleishig took me to the sauna in his hotel, after we changed clothes in his room. We were there for a few hours, and at the end of that time a man who looked like a laborer or a farmhand, who didn't speak Dutch, came into the sauna and saw us together. Sunday morning, the same man tried to knife me when I was on an errand for Fleishig. He had asked me to take photographs of the interior of the Portuguese synagogue, and when I left this man was waiting for me. It may not be enough evidence for the police, but it's enough for me.'

'And for me, Lodewijk. I have never heard anything like this.'

'That's not all. Around the time of the attack, someone walked into my apartment in New York with a set of keys. I think that the killer was in Fleishig's hotel room while we were in the sauna and that he copied my keys. All that was taken was a tape from my answering machine, with rude messages from Fleishig, and some of my letterhead. The only sense I can make out of this is that Fleishig was going to have me killed, then forge an invoice for the de Witte for some low figure and pocket the difference.'

'Could be.'

'Don't ask me how, but last night I got the painting back. If

Fleishig was desperate enough to want to kill me over the weekend, when he had the painting, he must be even more desperate now. That's why I'm bringing the painting here and offering it to you for a price I hope you can easily say yes to. The whole problem will go away as soon as a notice appears in the newspapers announcing your acquisition of the painting. Fleishig may have been able to get away with a fake invoice with the executors of my estate, whoever they are — I really have to write a will one of these days — but he isn't stupid enough to think he can get the painting away from you with a document like that. In any case, I have some more paper with me, and I'll write you a formal offer. I'll also give you a copy of my aunt's consignment agreement and a copy of a letter I'll write to her from here telling her that the painting is on offer to you to the exclusion of any other buyer until your option expires. Does that sound secure enough?'

'I'm sorry to have to say that this museum — before my time, of course — has acquired objects from sellers with far less convincing stories than that, and with bigger guns on their tail than Mitchell Fleishig. That's not the problem. The problem is our procedure, which can drag on forever. This has cost us badly in the past. Fortunately, our acquisitions committee has a bit of a guilty conscience about it that I can play on. They meet here on Wednesday, and I'll try to railroad the de Witte right past them. I'll put it on top of the agenda, and make sure that I get a vote on it then and there. Our restorer can give me a quick report by then. Do you have a file on the painting?'

'No. It all went very quickly. But if you leave me in the library for an hour, I can put together a set of photocopies of all the literature and write a few paragraphs of my own.'

'That will be fine. Where can I reach you later?'

'I'll call you. I don't know where I'll be between now and Wednesday. If the acquisition goes through, can you get it in the papers the next day?'

'I'll line up the *L.A. Times* for Thursday. Don't want you

out there in the cold for a minute longer than necessary.'

Altstad called Triolo from the public phone in the hall of the museum.

'I always knew you were destined for greatness, Lodewijk, but I had no idea just how quickly you were going to reach the top. Also I did not know that you were going to take me with you, for which my gratitude knows no bounds. Do you know what we did yesterday evening? Let me tell you. According to my friend at Central Credit Clearance –– this is not an advertising slogan, I mean a friend — your Mr. Fleishig is in hock for over one and a half million dollars to one Beniamino Santangelo, who according to my friend at the organized crime unit of the L.A.P.D., is the crown prince of a Mafia family that is distinguished, even in the context of its own picturesque culture, for inventive and gratuitous violence. And according to me, it is not from a goon hired by Fleishig from whom we stole a painting which according to you is worth two or three million dollars, but from a Santangelo foot soldier. We have ripped off the mob, Lodewijk, and lived to tell the tale. Allow me to annotate that last remark. We have so far lived about fifteen hours since this act of heroism on behalf of your maiden aunt Juliana. How many more hours of life are given to us depends in the short run on our ability to make ourselves disappear. In the long run, it is a function of our success in removing ourselves from the magic circle in which Messrs. Santangelo and Fleishig are doing their dance and into which we made such a spectacular entry yesterday.'

'Jesus Christ!'

'Well put, amigo. My very thoughts. Can you amplify concerning our long-run prospects?'

'I think I have sold the painting to the Mitty. If all goes well, the sale will be reported in the *L.A. Times* on Thursday.'

'For Mr. Fleishig's sake, I hope that when the paper hits the stands he has a better fallback position than they know about at

Central Credit. Frankly, they were rather bearish on him. He also seems to have disillusioned his bank. In their estimation, he has nothing else to fall back on but his ass. When Fleishig falls, where does that leave us, assuming we live until Thursday? If you were a Mafioso, Lodewijk, with the Weltanschauung that comes with the territory, how sporting would you be about a couple of guys who lifted you for a non-trivial amount of lucre?'

'They know that the painting never belonged to Fleishig. They can't hold it against us that Fleishig tried to steal a painting from me.'

'Ah, methinks I detect one or two fallacies in your thinking. One, we are dealing with people with an underdeveloped sense of mine and thine. Two, whether or not Fleishig was stealing the painting from you or they were stealing it from him will make much less impression on them than the incontrovertible fact that we stole it from them. That little matter, I fear, irrespective of everything else, is going to stick in their craw.'

'So what do we do?'

'We run like hell. But before we do, we cast one melancholy gaze down the path not taken. The sensible path, which for that reason alone is not a thinkable option for the likes of Robin Hood and his merry man yours truly. And that is to rush the painting to Mr. Santangelo with your compliments and apologies for having stolen it. Try to soften his heart enough to forget about us. Then you bill Fleishig — or more probably his estate — and hope that the bankruptcy court allows you a nickel on the dollar.'

Altstad was quiet.

'But your aunt's painting, let alone her money, is more important than the lives of a few small people who were mortals anyway to begin with, right?'

Silence.

'Hello, hello, operator. I've been cut off.'

'What can I say? If you put it that way, I'm risking your life for the sake of my money.'

'Now, now, not so cynical. Don't forget, you're risking your life too. As well as throwing away Fleishig's. And who's talking about money? This is art, n'est-ce pas?'

'I don't know what to say.'

'In that case, I'll have to answer for you. I would not be party to such a craven undertaking. Mr. Santangelo is not the only one around here who has his pride. Besides, what would happen if he accepted your painting and declined your apologies? Then you would die feeling silly, which must be awful. Now you can die feeling righteous, which I have been told is what life is all about.'

Fleishig had taken the day off to go to the beach. He was sleeping on his stomach with his head half in the sand and could not breathe very well, but he was too tired to turn over. His head was pounding from the sun and he had hurt his wrist playing volleyball. Nearby was a hotdog stand with an outdoor telephone bell that kept ringing. Why didn't someone pick it up?

Lifting his head from the sand, he realized he had been dreaming. He was not on the beach, he was in his own backyard. He was very tired from all that flying, and had fallen asleep on a collapsed chaise longue, with his head pushed at an angle into the grass, one eye jammed shut. Beatrice or the girl would get the phone. They knew he needed rest.

The phone kept ringing and Fleishig thought he had better answer it himself. He reached for the portable phone on the table next to the chaise longue. A jab of intense pain in his left wrist jarred him. He started spasmodically and his free eye unglued. It did not see grass. He was not in his backyard. He had no idea where he was.

Then he remembered. Santangelo said they were going to kill him if he didn't talk. The other two hit and kicked him as he tried to tell them about Altstad's painting. They didn't believe him and pushed a gun into his open eye. He did not know what happened next.

With his right arm he lifted himself to a sitting position. His left hand was hanging loosely and hurting unbelievably. He thought that his wrist must be broken. When his right eye started to focus, he saw that the pillow was covered with blood. His nose was clogged with dry blood and he had the feeling that there was blood all over his face and in his mouth. His left eye was swollen shut.

The telephone was on a night table at the head of the bed, still ringing. Fleishig shifted his leaden mass toward it. The touch of the horn convinced him that he was really awake. He wished he wasn't.

'You play dead on me, prick, and I'll join the game.'

'I was dead asleep.' Fleishig could not recognize his own voice or understand his words.

'Get in shape. In ten minutes you're going to call your wife, and you have to sound human. Or as human as you ever were. Get on your feet and get washed. Practice talking. Practice telling her that you are back in Palm Springs to close the deal you were working on and that you don't know how long it will take. Tell her to watch the office and cancel your appointments for the day. Ask her for messages, especially from the people who stole your painting. I'm going to give you a telephone number for those people to call. It's my lawyer, they can talk to him.'

Ten minutes later they called again and Fleishig did what they said. Beatrice was relieved to hear from him but suspicious of his story.

'Mitchell, why don't you give me a number where I can reach you?'

'The people I'm staying with are touchy that way. They don't want anyone to have their number. I don't even know it.'

'Is there anything wrong? You don't sound right.'

'No, nothing's wrong.' Why hadn't he told Beatrice what he was involved in? Not about Altstad but about the mob. If she knew more, maybe she would understand what was happening and perhaps do something about it. Now it was too late to tell her the truth. Thursday, when he could have told her, he had been too embarrassed. How sad. Husbands, he thought, confide in your wives. They understand you better than you think. There was a click on the line.

'Now say good-bye, stronzo.' Click.

'Beatrice?'

'I'm still here.'

'I love you, darling. Good-bye.' Click. She did not get a chance to reply.

Altstad left the Chevy in the parking lot of the L.A. County Fairgrounds, put the keys and a hand-drawn map in the mail to Triolo and caught a shuttle to Ontario International Airport. The first flight leaving was for Phoenix. He took it. Not until he was airborne did he remember what had happened to him the day before on the flight from Amsterdam. It did not recur. Without fear of falling, he landed at Sky Harbor in a little over an hour.

He rented a red Chrysler and followed the traffic onto the highway. At a suburban mall he bought a duffel bag, a week's worth of shirts, socks and underwear, Levi's, Nikes, a lined jacket, a baseball cap with no insignia, a two-person dome tent, a sleeping bag and air mattress, a small backpack, a camping kit, shaving and washing gear, paper towels, two gallons of drinking water and a fifth of tequila, twenty cans of rice and beans and corn and chili, two boxes of muesli, milk powder, a bag of dried apricots, a string of jerky, a map and a camper's guide to Arizona, a few paperbacks, six cassettes of bluegrass and country music and all the Bach cantatas in stock. He spent over six hundred dollars on a credit card. If the Reynolds and Mitty came through, he was a millionaire and could afford it. If they didn't, he was bankrupt and wouldn't have to pay anyway.

With cruise control at 65 and Flatt and Scruggs on four speakers, Altstad headed north on Interstate 17. He drove just as happily across the scrub and grit outside Phoenix as through the grand, green Prescott National Forest. At Flagstaff he got onto the 89. He did not stop until he reached Cameron, where he studied the guidebook over a Navajo stew with fry-bread. It was dark when he left the trading post, and a ghostly new moon was setting into what the map told him was the Grand Canyon. He filled the tank and took off in the opposite direction, toward the interior of the Navajo Reservation. Between Tuba City and Kayenta he found the left turn he wanted. At ten o'clock he pulled quietly into the camping ground of the Navajo National Monument. Only one site was taken, by a Ford pickup truck. He chose the spot at the bottom of the loop, furthest from the ranger's cabin. When he got out of the car he was rushed by the smell of pine.

As amazingly simple as it was to set up the tent, doing it nonetheless gave Altstad the satisfied feeling of having built his own house. When he turned off the headbeams, the silence grew quieter and the clean air purer. He poured himself half a cup of tequila and sat on the picnic bench near his tent, leaning back against the table and stretching his legs contentedly.

The morning before he went for a walk in his neighborhood in Amsterdam to take some photos for a customer, and now he was hiding from the Mafia on an Indian reservation in Arizona. Definitely a departure from the daily rut.

Altstad finished the tequila. By the dim starlight that reached him through the foliage he inflated his air mattress, undressed and got into his new sleeping bag. As he fell asleep he had the sensation that his head was being held firmly between two hands.

Altstad was woken by a rough voice saying 'We gotta leave right away. Better get up, mister.' By the time he got out of the tent, no one was around. He went to the toilet and tried to take a shower, but there was no water. It was cold, nearly freezing.

He dressed, ate a bowl of muesli, apricots and milk and cleaned up. Half an hour after the unknown visitor had announced their imminent departure, he returned. A stocky Indian man about fifty years old, barrel-chested and big-bellied, decked out in turquoise and silver, called out to him from the road.

'You ready?'

'What for?'

'For Keet Seel.'

'I think you're mistaking me for someone else.'

'You're not the guy Timothy called about?'

'No. I don't know any Timothy. Are you the ranger?'

'Do I look like a goddamn ranger?'

'I don't know. I just want to camp out here for a few days.'

'The place is closed. I opened the gate to let in some guy Timothy called about. If you're not him, forget it and go away. When I close the gate, you can't get out with your car.'

'Then I'd better get out now. Too bad, it's beautiful here.'

The Indian did not move. Altstad opened the duffel bag and started putting in his gear.

'You know what, I'll give you a special deal. Timothy said the guy would pay two hundred dollars for Keet Seel. I'll take you for one hundred.'

The day of reading, walking and napping Altstad had been looking forward to was not to be. Worse than that, he lost the comfortable feeling that he was out of sight in a benign spot where no one would think of looking for him. His imagination raced. The Indian would call Timothy and describe him and give him the license plate number of his car. Santangelo will have cast his nets wide for unusual travellers, and Timothy would report on him. How long could Altstad hide in unknown territory where he stood out as boldly as the Slav in the sauna?

A minute ago he had been a nameless tourist and now he was an exposed fugitive. Was he any safer going into a canyon with this suspicious-looking Indian? Maybe not, but he was at the man's mercy anyway, and going with him would at least keep him away from the telephone.

For half an hour they walked an easy trail skirting the rim of the canyon. They were in the shade of rustling leafy trees, and the air was pleasantly cool. The Indian stopped at a tall bush.

'Squawbush. The summer berries make great juice, better than Coke.' He broke off a stem and peeled the bark away. 'The women used to make baskets from the stem. Real high quality.'

He pulled down a branch from one of the trees under which they were walking.

'This here is juniper. Funny little leaves. Good bark, warm lining in winter and soft enough to keep a baby's ass dry. You got babies?'

'No. I'm not married.'

'You should marry, have babies. It would make you very happy. But to have babies you need a wife, and a wife makes you happy and unhappy. The juniper tree has the cure. The berries give a good taste to home-still. Helps you forget about your wife.' The Indian gave a huge grin, revealing a cave of golden stalagmites and stalactites at irregular intervals.

'Where I come from we also use juniper berries to flavor alcohol. Dutch gin.'

'Dutch? Where you from then?'

'Holland.'

'Overseas, right?'

'Yes. In Europe.'

'I been overseas. Vietnam.'

He stooped at a flower with a burst of long, spiky leaves and a single green shaft, thrusting out of it high and thin like a scraggly miniature Christmas tree.

'Yucca is good for everything. The leaves make rope and baskets.' Breaking one off, he let Altstad feel how sharp it was. 'Sewing needle in an emergency.' He pulled a plant out of the ground and twisted the roots until a drop of milky sap fell into Altstad's palm. 'Soap. Shampoo.' Fingering the small flowers, he told Altstad that they produced a fruit you could eat raw or roast or grind into meal.

They left the rim and began switchbacking down the canyon wall. The temperature shot up when they came out of the shade and rose steadily the lower they went. The guide raised a cloud of dust that forced Altstad to stay one turn behind him. There was no mistaking the path, but Altstad didn't dare stop to admire the view.

The floor of the canyon was not as green as it looked from above. Each plant and shrub stood alone, having made its own accommodation with the surroundings. They were not interchangeable members of a population, like the plants at the rim. The guide led Altstad to the shade of an overhanging cliff closed off with a fence.

'We wait here.' They drank water from their canteens and Altstad ate some apricots. A touchingly delicate green lizard ran past him. The sharp, dry air had a dusty tang that reminded him of the Sinai Desert. In this place he had never heard of and had not sought he felt strangely at home.

'Holland. Is that the country with water everywhere, even in the middle of the city?'

'That's it.'

'I seen a movie from Holland. Some Christian guy showed it at Window Rock. There were people being chased, they were not Christians, and the Christians saved them. It was during some war, maybe Korea.'

'It was World War Two, right?'

'Maybe. Who were you fighting?'

'The Germans.'

'Yeah, that's the war. The Germans were chasing these people who were not Christians, and the Christians let them hide in their houses and protected them. Many Christians were killed.'

'That isn't exactly how it went. The people being chased were the Jews. That's my people. Some of us were protected by the Christians, but most of us were not. Almost my whole family was killed by the Germans. Not many Christians were killed for protecting Jews.'

'So that Christian guy was telling a big lie.'

'He was twisting the facts.'

'That does not surprise me one bit.' The Indian laughed long and hard. 'They lie to my people about your people while both of us are dying and they survive.' He could not stop laughing.

Altstad laughed with him. Comparisons between the German attempt to exterminate the Jews and other tragedies generally irritated him. They always seemed to be capitalizing on the fame of the so-called Holocaust for some political purpose. It cheapened the suffering of the Jews and of whoever they were being compared with. This time he had a different reaction. He was embarrassed that the Jews, who were doing so well in the world, were being equated with an Indian tribe that had been decimated and demoralized and would never be the same as before its enemies came on the scene, enemies that included Jews. The Jewish way of life was not dependent on the land — not even the land of Israel — the way the Indian way of life was on a land that was lost to them forever. Their dead millions would not be replenished, their culture would never again function normally. But his guide was able to stand back and appreciate the correspondence between the Jews and the Indians at a level that had nothing to do with culture or land or history. It was the irony in the game of losing and winning that got to him. To a loser irony is funny. Winners hate it. But life is full of irony. If you ignore it, it defeats you. Who will have the last laugh?

A boy of about ten rode up on a blanketed small dapple gray,

holding a larger saddled brown horse in tow. The guide helped
Altstad into the saddle and struggled onto the boy's mount with
surprising difficulty. They headed off at a walk, the boy trailing
along behind them. After a mile or so, they turned into a nar-
rower side canyon. Not far from the mouth, they crossed a wash
running wild on the sandy floor from a waterfall in the canyon
wall. On the other side, behind a copse of cottonwood trees, was
a six-sided wooden house of a type Altstad had never seen before.

'My aunt's hogan. She always has nice things to sell.'

The boy went inside and came out with two little girls and an
older woman. The girls had strings of small rounded bale-shaped
beads draped over their forearms.

'Juniper berry seeds. Just right for a drunken Dutchman. For
tourists, they cost two dollars apiece. But on today's special deal,
you can have your pick for one dollar apiece.'

The beads were very simple and attractive. Altstad bought ten
strings, amazed at how cheap they were. The girls skittered away
giggling. Then the guide called over his aunt. She was wearing
silver and turquoise necklaces and bracelets. Encouraged by the
price of the beads, he asked to see the largest necklace the woman
was wearing. She took it off and handed it up to him. Some
twenty uneven chunks of polished turquoise alternating with
hollow silver rods opening horn-shaped at the end were strung
on heavy horsehair on either side of the central pendant. This
was a crescent-shaped silver medallion holding a large, smooth
convex turquoise plaque. The guide and his aunt shared an exchange in Navajo.

'That is an old piece. Pomegranate. Eight-and-a-half thousand dollars.'

Altstad, trained to show a poker face when hearing a price,
did not express surprise. But he realized he was out of his league.

'That is more than I can spend. How about that bracelet?'

He pointed at a thin silver bracelet, incised with a simple
lozenge design and inset with five oval turquoises. The Indians
went into conclave again.

'Do you have a girlfriend?'

'Yes.'

'This is for her. It was given to my aunt's mother by her husband's family before the wedding. Pretty good marriage, lots of children. Four hundred dollars.'

'Is that the special price?'

'Of course it's a very special price for you. But I tell you what, if you promise to give it to your girlfriend, we say three hundred twenty dollars. Eighty dollars is my wedding present to you.'

This was salesmanship of a high order, worthy of Willem Molenaar. Altstad saw no way out without losing face.

'I don't know if I have enough cash.'

'No problem. She takes MasterCard, Visa, Diners Club — you name it. A personal check with credit card is okay too.'

They closed the deal and Altstad put the bracelet into a zipper compartment in his backpack. He felt good about the purchase. His instinct told him he had not paid too much, and he was sure that Katy would like the bracelet.

The ride up the canyon was spectacular. His guide told him incomprehensible stories about the waterfalls and rock formations. It was hard to understand him, and he used words Altstad had never heard. The sun was high, and Altstad was feeling light-headed and a bit faint. He was thinking about asking if they could stop when the canyon narrowed into a shady defile, at the end of which the guide dismounted. From nowhere the boy appeared and took the reins as Altstad threw his leg over the horse's back and climbed down. The guide took a watermelon from a pouch in his saddlebag and gave instructions to the boy, then led Altstad onto a path cutting up the side of the canyon. Altstad trudged stiffly along behind him, hurting in unaccustomed places. He caught up with the guide at the foot of a tall ladder disappearing to a ledge on the canyon wall.

'You first,' the guide said.

With the guide holding onto the ladder, Altstad climbed unsteadily into the blue. He did his best not to show nervousness, but a glance down from halfway up started him trembling. When he reached the second rung from the top he panicked at the thought of taking the last step standing up straight with no handhold, and crawled onto the ledge on his elbows. Out of sight, he continued crawling until he was well away from the edge. As he got to his feet, he saw a sight which took his breath away. He was in the middle of a vast overhanging half-dome into which an abandoned city was built, stretching right and left as far as he could see. His mouth fell open. The squared-off buildings were the color of the cliff and he could not tell where construction ended, or if the buildings were hacked out of the rock.

There was a thud behind him and something hit the back of his legs. He shrieked and jumped into the air and almost came down on the watermelon that the guide had tossed onto the ledge from the ladder. The Indian stepped onto the ledge, giving no sign of having seen Altstad's scare. He sat down on the threshold of a house and cut up the watermelon. Altstad put away half of it with hardly a pause between slices. He knew he had not been drinking enough. While eating he walked back and forth on the ledge, looking in amazement at the cubic houses. The place had the mysterious air of having been abandoned suddenly, with the porridge still on the table. He couldn't blame the inhabitants for not wanting to live that remotely, in a place where they had to climb that miserable ladder a few times a day. But there were signs of recent repair. They couldn't have been gone long.

On his haunches he entered the house where the guide was sitting. The light, reflected through the small opening, had a russet glow much warmer than the world outside, and the air was cooler. The walls were made of dried mud, with a clay lining that needed touching up. The interior looked as if it could have been modelled by Henry Moore.

'Does this town belong to your people?'

'Keet Seel? Nah. It's an enemy town.'

'Why did the people leave? Did you drive out the enemy or was it the white man?'

'Neither. It was the spirits.'

'Did you ever visit it when it was occupied?'

'When people lived here, you mean?'

'Yes.'

The guide looked at Altstad strangely.

'Keet Seel been dead for seven hundred years.'

Altstad wobbled on his heels. For a moment he could not think. It was as if he had taken a wrong turn in an Escher print come to life. What entered his head as he steadied himself was a memory of his first trip to Los Angeles, four years earlier. Triolo had taken him to the tourist sights. On a visit to the mission of San Juan Capistrano, they had walked in a pious hush through the cloister and the primitive living quarters of the monks. The antiquity of the place evoked a seductive vision of what the continent had been like before the industrial revolution and manifest destiny. Altstad cherished a sensation of the remote past until he realized with a jolt that San Juan Capistrano was a century younger than his own house, which stood on a block that had hardly changed in four hundred years. Now he was in a town that had been abandoned before Amsterdam was built, and it looked new.

'This is a Pueblo III town, like in Mesa Verde and Canyon de Chelly.'

'I don't know those places. This is the first time I have ever been anywhere in the west except Los Angeles.'

'The first time in the west, in Keet Seel?'

'I'm afraid so.'

'You never heard of the Anasazi?'

'No.'

The guide shook his head.

'You must be the first one ever to visit Keet Seel without knowing about the Anasazi. Mostly, this is the last place, after they been everywhere else. Man, I got to tell you everything. Anasazi, that means enemy ancestors. Enemy of the Navajo, my people.'

The guide showed Altstad around the ruin, pointing out the

box-like houses for sleeping and storage, the garbage and burial areas behind them, and the round ceremonial spaces called kivas. He told him how the Anasazi farmed the canyon floors from villages perched halfway up the cliffs. Many Anasazi skeletons, he said, had broken bones.

When they got to the opposite end of the ledge, in the shade, there was a pan of chili, fry-bread, bowls and spoons and full canteens waiting for them.

'Isn't the boy going to eat with us?'

'He's shy, doesn't speak English yet. He'll take care of himself.'

The guide talked as they ate.

'The west is very dry, partly desert. Before pumps and pipelines, Indians had to know every place in the country where there was water. Streams and rivers, but also springs, drybed arroyos, pools of runoff rainwater. They are all part of the system of mountains and rivers. The rivers here are the Colorado, the Little Colorado, the San Juan and the Rio Grande. We are at the edge of the basin of the San Juan, which empties into the Colorado River where Lake Powell is now. The San Juan gathers water from big rivers in Colorado and small rivers and arroyos in New Mexico and Arizona. The enemy ancestors lived everywhere in the whole region and in the Little Colorado basin to the south. They liked the high mesas, four, five thousand feet, going up to eight thousand feet sometimes. Cooler, wetter, safer.

'First they lived in dugouts. Basketmaker II culture, Basketmaker III. Very simple, small groups, what they call subsistence living. Then they got fancy, you know what I mean? They moved into the canyons and built villages, then towns like Keet Seel. This only lasted a short time. Keet Seel is on the last arroyo going into the San Juan, and the shortest. They were getting kind of desperate. Archaeologists did carbon dating, they found that all of Keet Seel was built in a short time in the late twelve hundreds. It was started in like 1250 and they stopped building in 1282. Then they disappeared. The Pueblo Indians on the Rio Grande and the Zuñi and Hopi in the Little Colorado basin say they are descendants. Maybe they are.

'Anyway, by the time my people came, the enemy ancestors were gone. We found their houses, but we didn't live in them. Do you want to know why they left?'

'Of course.'

'Sure, everybody wants to know. The archaeologists have lots of reasons. They have schools. Whatever kind of person they are, they find a school to join. The population grew too fast. There was an epidemic. The water table fell. The game disappeared. They overworked their fields. Crop disease. Diet deterioration.

'Diet deterioration, that is my favorite. The enemy ancestors knew more about living off this land than anybody. They could make food and medicine out of a hundred different trees and plants and bushes. You got to listen to some guy who grew up on Big Macs and fries saying the enemy ancestors didn't know how to feed themselves. When I took the guide course at the University of New Mexico, they told me this. They also told me that the Anasazi were driven away by enemies. They were a peaceful society, with no leaders, they said. Can you imagine? No leaders. I have it in a book, you don't have to believe me. So they couldn't defend themselves. Or they had a civil war.

'That's supposed to explain why every single last enemy ancestor left the San Juan basin in about ten years before 1300 and then went to the Rio Grande or the Little Colorado as a smaller population than here. No one tells you why, if they were shrinking anyway because of all those reasons, they didn't stay where they were. Or why some didn't stay when enough of the others had left.

'You invent a reason for the great migration — the crazier the better — and I will give you the name of an archaeologist who already said it. I still have the books from the course.'

The guide was worked up. Altstad sympathized with him. He recognized this kind of reasoning from art history, and he got indignant about it too. But it was not only the guide's intellect that was insulted. He was outraged in his beliefs.

'Maybe white men change country for reasons like that. Not

Indians. The Indian reason is different. We Navajo believe that the enemy ancestor was driven out by the spirits. The earth is our mother, and she lets us live off her. But no one has the right to claim her for themselves. That was the sin of the enemy ancestors. Look how they dug themselves into the creases of mother earth. You don't do that. They were punished. Over at Canyon de Chelly you can see where they were burned out. The whole canyon was destroyed by fire. Just about everybody was killed, and whoever wasn't killed got the message and left. That is the reason.'

Altstad was fighting to keep his eyes open. The guide let him gently off the hook.

'Maybe you want to rest up before we go back. You want to come down with me or stay here?'

'I'm very tired. I think I'd better have a nap up here before I get back on the ladder.'

'That's okay for you. I would never sleep in an enemy ancestor town. But white men do it a lot.'

Altstad crept into a kiva and lay down on his back on the cool floor. When he closed his eyes he saw a beautiful young woman, completely black, as bright as a clear night sky. She was stretched out over him, her long raven hair forming a curtain between her upward-reaching arms. Although she was so close that her body pressed on his everywhere, he could nonetheless see her. She was naked, but what he felt was not the touch of her skin. It was as if her body merged into his, face into face, chest into chest, limbs into limbs. The thrill was overwhelming and would have killed him had he not sunk into the ground, leaving his body on the surface in its union with the woman. With every breath, he descended a few inches deeper into the earth. He knew that he was still feeling her flesh mingle with his, but his real self was at an increasing distance. The weight of his sunken self prevented him from moving.

As his eyes grew accustomed to the dark, he saw that deep in the woman's body stars were shining. The brightest one, in her belly, was spinning and growing. That must be her baby, Altstad thought. How wonderful. He would be just like a father to the child, even though he knew it was not his.

'I am going away, Lodewijk.'

Her voice filled the sky. It was made of music and the sounds of nature. Altstad wanted to tell her to stay, but he could not speak.

The vision began to move away, filling Altstad with unbearable sadness. She lowered her arms, bringing the curtain of her hair down over her face. She turned around and extended her right hand. It was grasped by the left hand, a white hand, of someone else. As she receded, the figure of her companion appeared. It was Altstad's father! He was walking away, taking her with him.

Altstad tried to call out, but still could not make a sound. His father seemed to hear him, though. He stopped and turned around. His father looked just like Lodewijk remembered him. Jan Mark was wrong.

'Hello, son.'

'Hello, pappie.'

'I'm going away now.'

'Do you have to?'

'Yes. I should have gone a long time ago, but you didn't want me to.'

'I want you with me always, pap.'

'That can't be. When a person dies, they should go away. When I died, you wouldn't let me go. You didn't cry, you know.'

'I know. I always felt terrible about that.'

'It wasn't your fault. I taught you how not to mourn. You had to learn yourself, by losing something of your own.'

'You're just like I remember you. I'll always remember you, pap.'

'That's nice. I'm glad. Now I'm going away with the stars in the sky.'

The stars had grown larger. Lodewijk turned to look at them and saw that they had the faces of his cousins and uncles and aunts and grandparents in Aunt Juliana's photographs. He tried to shift his gaze back to his father but could not. He wanted to say good-bye, but it was too late. All he could see were the stars, millions of them now, each of them a face shining brilliantly in a living black sky. He was crying, with loud sobs. He cried uncontrollably until the sounds of his crying began to awaken him. They were no longer reverberating in space, they were echoing close by. The night sky had brightened unremarked into a gentle orange dawn. His body was back on the kiva floor, the weight had lifted and he could move again. As he woke, he heard the echo of his last sob. The earthen floor was wet with his tears.

The Indian had a hot drink ready for him when he climbed down the ladder.

'This is a brew from a special root that only grows in these canyons. People drink it when they have seen a spirit. I think maybe you saw a spirit.'

That night, Altstad slept as he had never slept before. He closed his eyes as he began to turn onto his side, and opened them again as he rolled onto the other side, in what seemed like a continuous motion. Only now it was morning, and he was exhilaratedly awake and fresh. He laughed out loud in delight.

Altstad breakfasted, put his things in the car, and left. He took highway 180 into Tuba City and got on the phone to Jackson Hampshire.

'Lodewijk, I hope you are not going to be very disappointed.'

No, only very dead, thought Altstad, if the sale did not go through.

'I was afraid that the committee would balk at two and a half million. That would have been a record price for a de Witte, and we do what we can to avoid setting new records. So I told them it was on offer for two million. And they gave me carte blanche. Can you live with that?'

'That's the right word. Yes, I think I can.'

'I'm glad. Because I went around internal channels and gave an interview to the *L.A. Times* on condition that it appears in tomorrow's paper, and that it names you as the seller. If you turned down the offer, I would probably have more explaining to do than people would understand.'

'Jackson, I'll never forget that you did this for me. Thank you.'

Altstad's next call was a long talk with Los Angeles International Airport. Then he dialed Fleishig's office. His wife answered.

'Mr. Altstad, I can't tell you how happy I am that you're calling. I think you're the only one who can get through to Mitchell. I'm very worried about him. He hasn't been home since Sunday. He called Monday morning to say he had to be in Palm Springs on business and asked me to watch the office. I didn't like the way he sounded. He left a telephone number for you. I tried it, but they wouldn't speak to me. His bank is also trying to get in touch with him. There is something very wrong going on and I feel completely helpless.'

She gave him a name and an L.A. telephone number. He

promised to let her know as soon as he had news of Mitchell. Then he hung up and dialed the number.

'Bianco and Robbins, attorneys-at-law.'

'May I speak to Mr. Robbins, please.'

'Who is calling?'

'This is Lodewijk Altstad. He's expecting my call.'

'Hold on please, Mr. Altstad.'

Robbins kept him waiting for two minutes. Let them trace the call, thought Altstad.

'Thomas Robbins.'

'This is Lodewijk Altstad. I got your number from Mitchell Fleishig's wife.'

'Where are you calling from, Mr. Altstad?'

'From a phone booth a thousand miles from L.A., which I'm leaving as soon as I put down the phone.'

'I see. What is the purpose of your call?'

'To establish contact with Beniamino Santangelo.'

'Mr. Santangelo is my client. What is it that you want from him?'

'I believe there is something he wants from me. I'd like to talk to him about it.'

'Can you be more concrete?'

'Yes, I can. I would like to speak to Mr. Santangelo *and* Mr. Fleishig about the painting. Tomorrow morning at LAX. I would appreciate it if you would ask them to be in the ground-floor entrance hall to Terminal 5 between 7:30 and 8 am. During that time I will contact Mr. Santangelo, but only if he is in the company of Mitchell Fleishig.'

'If you don't mind my saying so, this is rather a rude kind of invitation for someone of Mr. Santangelo's stature. I am sure he would rather meet you at his office or here during normal business hours.'

'No impoliteness intended, Mr. Robbins, but those are my conditions. Would you mind repeating them?'

'Ground-floor entrance hall to Terminal 5 at LAX tomorrow morning between 7:30 and 8.'

'You're forgetting one essential.'

'And that is?'

'Mr. Santangelo must be accompanied by Mr. Fleishig. Is that understood?'

'I will see to it that Mr. Santangelo gets your message. Where can I reach you to confirm the appointment?'

'It's kind of you to offer, but that won't be necessary. If the gentlemen do not show up, I will draw my own conclusions.'

Altstad made one more call, to Triolo's answering service, asking him to be at Terminal 6 at a quarter after seven Thursday morning with a copy of the morning's *L.A. Times*, and looking presentable.

In Phoenix, Altstad found a family camping ground which did have water in the showers. He washed and shaved and got a few hours of sleep. One of these days he really had to start following Jan Mark's advice and get more rest, he thought. Maybe tomorrow, if he survived the morning.

Dressed in clean new clothes, he dropped off the car at Sky Harbor at 5:30 in the morning and made the 6 o'clock flight to Los Angeles. As airport information had told him, the plane docked at Terminal 6. Triolo was not there. Altstad walked straight for a telephone to try his service again. If anything had happened to Triolo, he would get on the next plane out. As he started to dial, he felt a dig in the ribs and froze.

'We got the papers. You got the money?'

'*Godverdomme*, Sy, God damn you. At a moment like this?'

'It was that "be presentable" that did it. Made something snap inside me. Anyway, mazeltov, boychik. I read the paper. Our stolen painting has been laundered whiter than white.'

'How often do I have to tell you it's not stolen?'

'Just keep saying it until I say when. But what does that matter? It's not me you have to convince, it's Mr. Santangelo.'

'Right. That's why I arranged to meet him here.'

'Here?'

'Yes.'

'When? Not now, by any chance?'

'Yes, now. Between 7:30 and 8.'

'Lodewijk, if I may say so, I have a certain reputation among those who know me for scorning danger. I think the time has come for me to reveal to you the secret of my technique. What I do is follow danger at a certain distance, and when I have a clear escape route I shout "Hey danger, naah, nah-nah, naah, naah," stick out my tongue and then duck around a corner and run. You, on the other hand, who have the name of being a quiet, conventional type of person — I'm sorry if I am the first to tell you this — have developed a style with danger which puts mine utterly to shame. This is the second occasion in a short period in which I have been privileged to observe you in operation. What you do is walk up to danger, grab it by the lapels and spit in its face. With utter disregard for your own safety and, if you don't mind my saying it, for my own. Why, Lodewijk, tell me why?'

'You said yourself we had to get out of the Santangelo-Fleishig circle. Well, if Santangelo kills Fleishig the circle will be made immortal and we may never escape. So I'm going to try to break the circle before that happens. I'm doing it to get us *out* of danger, Sy. All I want you to do is see if they're here. They're supposed to be in the middle of the entrance to terminal 5. None of them knows you. Just have a look around. I expect Santangelo to have men posted to pick me up and put me in a car before I can reach him. So I won't enter from the street. My idea is to walk from 6 to 5 one level up and come down to the arrival hall in 5 by the stairs from above. I need you to let me know if you think I can reach them that way. Will you do it?'

'It's not far out of my way, why not?'

Triolo left at 7:35, and Altstad did not think he needed more than ten minutes to walk his round. At 7:45 there was no sign of him. Altstad moved closer to the front door, half expecting to see Triolo being dragged off. It was ten to eight, then eight to eight, and finally Triolo came through the doors of Terminal 6.

'The coffee in Terminal 5 is shocking.'

'Sy, have a heart. I only have a few minutes. Please.'

'Well, if I must. A trauma case looking like your Mr. Fleishig is in the middle of the hall, in the company of a small smart fellow who fits my cliché image of a California mafioso. While drinking the coffee I sacrificed myself to swallow on your behalf, I checked out the backup squad. I must say, Lodewijk, that you may have missed your métier. Santangelo has two men on the street entrance and one on each ground-floor corridor. If you came from either of those three sides, you would never reach him. But if you make a break from upstairs, you have a chance of getting to him before they march you out of the front door to God knows where. One nice touch is that there's a security desk at the upper level.'

'Keep an eye on the ground-floor exit of Terminal 5, Sy. If they take me, go to the police.'

With two minutes to go, Altstad ran upstairs. He dashed to Terminal 5, a glittering new marble-and-glass construction. From the upper hall, he could see Fleishig and Santangelo in the middle of an inlaid circle of brown-and-beige marble tiles. Glancing at the security guard behind him, he called out into the hall, forcing himself to shout at the top of his lungs:

'Mitchell Fleishig and Beniamino Santangelo. Mitchell Fleishig and Beniamino Santangelo, what a coincidence. Just the men I wanted to see. I have a flight in ten minutes, but let's have a talk right here.'

With everyone in the terminal staring at him, Altstad rushed downstairs to Fleishig and shook the hand that was not in the sling. Santangelo's men were looking to their boss for guidance. He motioned them to hold back, and turned to Altstad fuming.

'What the fuck are you trying?'

'To have a talk with you, Mr. Santangelo. I'm the one who took the painting outside Fleishig's house Sunday afternoon.'

'I know that. And I know you were not alone. I have nothing to talk to you about except to tell you to bring me the painting and the other guy. Then maybe we'll talk.'

'That painting was mine to sell, not Mr. Fleishig's. He had no business offering it to you. In any case, I have sold it. It is irretrievable even for you.'

Altstad had the newspaper in his hand. He showed the story of the acquisition to Santangelo.

'So you sold it to the Mitty. All the worse for you and your buddy, and much, much the worse for Mr. Fleishig here.'

Fleishig was groggy. He was looking at the ground. When he heard what Santangelo said, he started shaking.

'What is it you want, Mr. Santangelo? The painting? Fleishig? Or your money?'

'If Fleishig was able to pay me my money, we wouldn't be in this situation, right?'

'Suppose Fleishig does pay you?'

'Fleishig isn't worth a fucking cent. Those paintings you sold him, which he used as collateral, aren't worth a fucking cent.'

'How much did you lend him on those paintings?'

'One and a half million,' Santangelo muttered in embarrassment. 'With interest, he now owes me almost one point nine.'

'If he paid you, would you let him go?'

'Of course I would. But what kind of shit-eating question is that? The guy is worth nothing.'

'If he paid you, would you call it quits between us as well?'

'Why should I? You attacked one of my men in the street and robbed him.'

'Mr. Santangelo, I think you understand why I did that, and I think you would have done the same under the circumstances. I apologize for hurting your man. I think I can trust your good will on that matter, if the loan is paid back. That's what I came to talk to you about.'

'So talk.'

'The Mitty never announces what it pays for acquisitions. I'll tell you. They're paying two million dollars. I am prepared to have the full amount of Fleishig's debt paid to you directly by the museum. I will take over the loan.'

Santangelo was flabbergasted. He could not make sense out of what he was hearing. He gave it one try.

'You think the paintings are worth that much?'

'That's my business.'

No, Altstad must know as well as he did that at auction the paintings wouldn't fetch much more than twenty percent of the loan.

'What are you pulling? You expect me to believe that you broke cover to give almost two million dollars to a man who tried to kill you? Don't you know that Fleishig put a mark on you for no reason except to get that painting cheap?'

'I know.'

'That is subhuman behavior. I never heard of anything like it. Do you hear what I am saying? *I* never heard of such a thing.'

'He was very frightened.'

'And I never heard of anyone doing what you're doing. Are you some kind of saint?'

'I just want everyone to walk away from this situation in one piece.'

'That is more important to you than one point nine million dollars?'

'I would like to live the rest of my life at peace with myself, and that may be difficult if I stood back now, knowing that I am the only person in the world who can save Fleishig.'

Santangelo looked hard at Altstad.

'Is he family to you?'

'No. But he's my best customer. He's the only one buying the paintings I was trying to build a market for. But that's not the point. I just decided for myself that no matter what happens, I'm not going to stand by and see someone killed if there's anything I can do about it.'

Santangelo waved his men back. With Altstad and Fleishig, he walked to a vacant counter. They filled out payment instructions on an invoice to the Mitty for two million dollars. Altstad put it into a stamped envelope addressed to Jackson Hampshire.

'This envelope is yours, Mr. Santangelo, if you agree to walk out of here without Fleishig. I trust you to respect my own safety and that of the second man. When the Mitty check passes, the slate will be wiped clean.'

'A clean slate,' Santangelo said softly. 'That would be worth more than a couple of million to me.'

He shook Altstad's hand and without looking at Fleishig took the envelope and walked away.

A minute later, Triolo was with them.

'Three stretch limos for five passengers. Those guys will never have money in the bank. Out of curiosity, Lodewijk, what did you do to get them into the cars?'

'I paid off Fleishig's debt. Speaking of which, let me write down the amount while it's fresh in my mind. One million eight hundred and twenty-two thousand five hundred dollars.'

He wrote it on two scraps of paper and gave one to Fleishig.

'This is what you owe me.'

'Sy, can I ask you one more favor?'

'Let me guess. The *Night Watch*, right? I'm your man.'

'Could you take Fleishig home for me? You know where he lives. Go inside with him, deliver him to his wife with my compliments and make sure he calls the man with the suntan in Amsterdam. I'm going to New York. I have a wedding present to deliver.'

'The strangest things happen when I don't write to you.'

In a padded red imitation leather booth in their favorite Second Avenue delicatessen, Altstad and Katy were rebuilding their relationship between bites of overstuffed pastrami and corned-beef with coleslaw three-decker combination sandwiches, with French fried potatoes washed down by Dr. Brown's Cel-ray Tonic.

He told her the story of Fleishig's scam. He told her how he had given nearly all the money from the sale of his aunt's painting to a gangster and how he now owed his aunt a million dollars. Fortunately, he was able to report that the Reynolds Museum of Art had offered him 800,000 dollars for the Jan Steen, so that he was a mere 200,000 dollars in the hole.

'And to think that I would have had all of this on paper as it was happening if I hadn't asked you not to write.'

'I have the feeling that if you hadn't, things may not have worked out this way. I was desperately holding on to that image of you, and I was desperately trying to make a lot of money. It was a stupid bet with myself. If you hadn't shaken me loose, I don't think I would have been able to buy Fleishig back. He would be dead and the mob would be after Sy and me.

'You were right to say that I was creating an unreal image of you. An idol may be more like it. I shouldn't worship it. I shouldn't worship you. Love is more than idol worship. What Emma Rae said was also right. Holding on to a very materialistic idea of art was part of my bet. I think I can relax now and let in things that I don't understand. Anyway, I called off the bet.'

'That's good. I wouldn't like to think that you won me on a bet.'

'Have I won you?'

'What do you think?'

'I think I want to be married to you. Katy, would you marry a helpless debtor who would lie to the *Kensington Journal*?'

Katy, caught by surprise while taking a bite out of a dill pickle, got some brine down the wrong pipe and started coughing and crying. Altstad moved over beside her and patted her on the back. As the coughing subsided he began caressing her and when it stopped he kissed her. She returned the kiss with feeling and then pulled back. She looked at him and looked around.

'You took me to Rubenstein's Famous to propose because you don't have a car, right?'

'Who needs a car in New York and Amsterdam? But if you want one, I'll get you one.'

'You dumb Dutchman, you know what I mean.'

'You mean you want to make love in this booth, don't you?'

He slipped a hand up to her breast and kissed her again. She pushed him away.

'Get back to your own seat before they kick us out of here.'

'Not until you give me your answer.'

Now she kissed him, talking between her teeth as she did.

'My answer, Lodewijk, is Yes.'

They let the kiss take its course.

'Then I have something for you.'

Altstad took the bracelet out of his jacket pocket.

'This is from me and from Joseph Largo of Kayenta, Arizona. He is a great admirer of yours, and he says this bracelet will bring us a happy marriage and lots of children.'

'It's beautiful. I love it. I love you.'

'I love you.

'Now that we're engaged, will you come to celebrate my thirtieth birthday next week?'

'Of course, why do you ask?'

'Because you'll have to come to Amsterdam to do it. I'll be serving tea and creampuffs at my mother's place. Something tells me she'd like to meet you.'

'I'd love to meet your mother.'

He took Katy's hands and looked into her eyes. They were black and deep as the night.

By afternoon visiting hours at Mt. Sinai Hospital, Fleishig
was in the ward, trussed and plastered, showing only one eye
and a mouth. The description of his condition on the clipboard
at the foot of the bed was three pages long. He had been beaten
'to within an inch of his life,' the doctor told Beatrice, sounding
as if he were impressed by such sensitive brinkmanship.

'So why didn't you tell me any of this?'

'I was too ashamed. Can you imagine how ashamed I was?'

'If what Mr. Triolo told me is right, and I believe him, you
weren't too ashamed to try to kill that nice Mr. Altstad. But you
were too ashamed to tell your own wife that you had money
troubles.'

'That's right. Crazy, isn't it? What can I say? I couldn't admit
to you that I had gotten us into such a mess. I was always proud
of being a good provider.'

'You thought I would want you to kill someone so I could live
in a nice house? Did you really think that of me?'

'No, of course not. It was me. I don't know what I was thinking. I was too desperate to think.'

'You're lucky you aren't dead. Mr. Altstad saved your life.'

'I know. How do you think that makes me feel?'

'He also could have you locked up in jail in Holland for the
rest of your life, and he isn't even pressing charges.'

'I'll make it up to him.'

'How can you ever do that? You try to kill someone and
then you say you'll make it up to them? There's something
seriously wrong with your sense of values, Mitchell. I'm sorry
I let you go your own way all these years. From now on you're
going to tell me all about everything you're doing. Anyway,

I'm glad at least that I can pay back Mr. Altstad what you owe him.'

'What do you mean, Bea? You don't have any money.'

'Yes, I do. I got it in the mail last Thursday. Look.'

She took a letter out of her handbag.

Dear Bea,

You probably noticed I was not very good at our canasta game this morning. The pain has gotten too bad, and I am going to take a cocktail at bedtime, if you know what I mean. Don't tell anybody, there's going to be questions anyway and I don't want no one to get into trouble. You are the nicest person I ever knew, and I feel bad about winning all that money from you at cards. I could leave it to you in my will, but there's no time and you would have to wait too long. So here's a check to cover your losses plus taxes if they make you pay but I don't think you should. The bank manager at Wells Fargo, Mr. Chapkis, knows about it, just go straight to him and you won't have to tell anybody. I love you and hope you have a wonderful healthy and long life.

Love,

Rachel

'So your friend Rachel paid you back what you lost playing cards with her? That's very touching. But do you have any idea what kind of money we're talking about? You think I went broke over canasta money?'

'Well, you see I thought we were just playing for points. I said dollars, for fun, and I had no idea she took it seriously. She must have been very rich and used to playing with other very rich people if she thought I could play for stakes like that. But I never paid her a penny in real money.'

'So how much is it?'

'Almost two million dollars.'

Fleishig sat up and hit his head against the lamp. The pain almost knocked him out.

'She sent you a check for two million dollars?'

'Three. She was afraid I would have to pay tax on it. But Mr. Chapkis said he didn't think anyone would ever know about it. The check was made out to Cash. He gave me bearer bonds and I put them right into a safe deposit box.'

Fleishig was trying to think.

'Thursday? So you had the check before I flew to Holland?'

'I didn't know you were flying to Holland. You told me you were going to Palm Springs, remember?'

'But you knew I was in trouble with the bank. That you knew.'

'You wouldn't tell me the truth about that. And you were very abusive, not just to me but also to Jeanie. I was able to straighten things out with her. She came back, but she's working for me now, not for us, so you have nothing to say about it. And I want you to apologize to her when you come home. I told her you were having a nervous breakdown. If you hadn't fired Jeanie without talking to me about it, maybe I would have told you about the check.'

'None of this had to happen,' Fleishig intoned. 'This whole thing did not have to happen.'

'That's right. If you were a nicer person, it would not have happened. I hope you learned your lesson. So how much did Mr. Altstad pay for you?'

'One million eight and change.'

'You give me his telephone number and I'll ask him how he wants the money.'

Fleishig was silent for a moment.

'I'm not sure we can do that.'

'How come?'

'We also owe the bank a lot of money. They have a prior claim.'

'It's my money. I never signed away my own money.'

'With three million, I would be back in business, and I could pay Lodewijk within a year or two.'

'Mitchell, how rotten can you be? You want to steal that money twice from Mr. Altstad.'

'Without it, I'm bankrupt.'

'So you're bankrupt. The way you're behaving, you deserve to be bankrupt. I'm glad. Maybe it will do you some good.'

'And your brother? If I go bankrupt, what do you think is going to happen to your precious brother I had to give a job to so badly? How do you think he'll like being on welfare?'

'Oh, I was going to tell you. Arnold quit. He called on Tuesday to say he closed the office and wasn't going back. He joined a chassidic community in upstate New York. They put him in charge of the hats and caps department of their co-op shop. He said I should thank you for him. You helped him become a penitent, he said. That's the only nice thing I've heard about you all week.'